ECHO

kate morgenroth

Also by Kate Morgenroth
Jude

ECHO

kate morgenroth

SIMON & SCHUSTER BOOKS FOR YOUNG READERS
New York   London   Toronto   Sydney

SIMON & SCHUSTER BOOKS FOR YOUNG READERS
An imprint of Simon & Schuster Children's Publishing Division
1230 Avenue of the Americas, New York, New York 10020
SIMON & SCHUSTER BOOKS FOR YOUNG READERS is a trademark of Simon & Schuster, Inc.
Book design by Daniel Roode
The text for this book is set in Cochin.
Manufactured in the United States of America
10 9 8 7 6 5 4 3 2
Library of Congress Cataloging-in-Publication Data
Morgenroth, Kate.
Echo / Kate Morgenroth. — 1st ed.
p. cm.
Summary: After Justin witnesses his brother's accidental shooting death, he must live with the repercussions, as the same horrific day seems to happen over and over.
ISBN-13: 978-1-4169-1438-9
ISBN-10: 1-4169-1438-2
[1. Death — Fiction. 2. Post-traumatic stress disorder — Fiction.] I. Title.
PZ7.M826695Ec 2007
[Fic] — dc22
2005032984

For my brother and sister

Prologue

"I think we have, like, the worst parents in the world," Mark said to his brother.

"Yeah?" Justin said, barely paying attention. He was lying with his feet up on the couch, reading a Daredevil comic book. It was a new couch—cream-colored suede. Their mother had just bought it last week, and their father's only comment was, "Do you think it's smart to get that color with two teenage boys in the house?" Justin would have been in big trouble if his mother had seen him with his sneakers propped up on the arm of the couch. But their mother wasn't home.

"Yeah. I mean, what kind of parents leave their twelve-year-old kid alone every afternoon?" Mark demanded.

"You're not alone," Justin pointed out. "I'm here."

"I just don't think you can provide proper supervision for me."

"Uh-huh," Justin said sarcastically, going back to his comic.

"I can't *believe* they did this to me." Mark kicked the side of the entertainment center. The entertainment center was also new, and it was the real reason Mark was upset. The bulky piece of furniture was stationed in a corner of the living room, and it housed the TV and the stereo. Their mother had gone to buy a couch, and had come home with this as well, because she had seen it displayed in the store with a sign propped up against it that read BETTER THAN THE V-CHIP. The entertainment center was made out of solid oak—and it was equipped with a heavy lock. Their mother had always *hated* it when they watched TV, but she hadn't been able to control how much they watched in the hours between when they got home from school and she returned home from work. Now she'd found a way.

At that moment the cabinet was shut and firmly locked.

"I'm gonna miss my show," Mark wailed. "They don't understand. I can't miss that show. Everyone watches it. *Everyone*. And tomorrow at school they're all gonna be talking about what happened, and I'm gonna look like a total dork. What if someone asks me about it? What am I gonna say?" Mark paused, waiting for an answer, but Justin just shrugged.

"Can you even believe they put a friggin' lock on the friggin' TV?" Mark demanded.

"Yeah," Justin said. "I can believe it."

In a high-pitched voice Mark mimicked, "It's for your own good. You boys watch too much TV." Then, back in his normal voice again, "I mean, did anyone ever tell her that too much is a relative term? Too much for one person may not be enough for another."

Justin lowered his comic and looked at Mark. "Yeah . . . but you do watch too much, you know."

Mark rolled his eyes. "But they don't understand. This is important. Shit." To punctuate his remark, Mark landed another kick against the side of the cabinet.

"There's nothing you can do about it," Justin said philosophically. He could afford to be philosophical—his favorite show was on later, when their parents would be home.

"Oh yeah?"

Justin heard something in his brother's tone, and he looked up just in time to see Mark heading out of the room.

"Where are you going?" Justin called after him. But Mark didn't answer.

Justin stared at the empty doorway for a moment, then went back to his comic.

Mark returned a few minutes later brandishing a screwdriver.

"Nothing I can do about it?" Mark taunted. "Is that what you said?"

Justin snorted. "You gotta be kidding me."

"Just you wait and see." Mark crossed to the entertainment center and knelt in front of it, carefully fitting the screwdriver into the lock.

"You're not gonna be able to open it," Justin said.

"Says you," Mark snapped. Then he attacked the lock.

Five minutes later Justin looked up at the sound of the screwdriver skidding across the floor. Mark had tossed it across the room, and had sat back on his heels.

Justin shook his head and went back to reading. A minute later he heard Mark get up, retrieve the screwdriver, and go back to work on the cabinet with redoubled intensity, muttering, "I'm gonna get this thing open."

"You won't," Justin said matter-of-factly.

After another furious attack on the lock, Mark let the screwdriver drop. "You're right," he said. "I'm not gonna get this thing open."

"Course I'm right," Justin said, but he was surprised that his brother would admit it.

"Yeah, but I know what I *can* get open," Mark said. And he stood up and left the room again.

"Where are you going?" Justin called. "Mark?" Justin stared at the empty doorway again for a few seconds. When his brother didn't reappear, he tossed aside the comic and followed. He found Mark in the upstairs hallway, outside their parents' bedroom, bent over the lock on their door, working at it with the same screwdriver.

Justin walked up behind him and peered over his shoulder. "You're not going to be able to open it," he said again, but hopefully this time.

"Oh yeah?" Mark straightened, turned the knob, and pushed the door open with a flourish.

Their parents' bedroom was large and reflected their mother's compulsive orderliness. The huge king-size bed had been made up without a wrinkle, there were no clothes lying around, no drawers open, and even the pillows looked like they'd been fluffed. But all Mark and Justin saw was the large flat-screen TV opposite the bed.

Justin stood in the doorway for a moment, not quite believing it. Suddenly he gave a whoop and ran in and dove onto the bed. Mark followed, belly flopping on top of him. Justin let out an exaggerated groan and heaved him off. They were both laughing.

"Where's the remote?" Justin asked, looking around. "You don't want to miss any of the show."

"Oh, shit." Mark scrambled off the bed and found the remote in the drawer of one of the bedside tables. "Figures it would be on Mom's side," he said, and flicked on the television.

An hour later Mark and Justin were stretched out, a glass of Coke on each bedside table, and a bag of chips on the bed between them. The bed itself was a mess. It was rumpled, with pillows tossed on the floor and propped under their feet. A few of the chips were spilling out onto the duvet and had left some faint grease stains. The TV was on, the sound turned up. Both boys had their eyes fixed on the screen, but Mark watched with especially intense concentration, almost as if he were hypnotized.

Justin reached over and picked up the remote, which was lying on the bed between them, and changed the channel.

"Hey," Mark protested, jarred from his trance. "Change it back."

"We watched your show," Justin pointed out. "Now I get to choose. And *TRL* is boring."

"I like *TRL*."

"Too bad. I'm couch commando."

"That's so not fair," Mark protested, pushing himself up. "I got the door open —"

"And I've got the remote," Justin finished.

"Not for long," Mark retorted, grabbing for it, but Justin playfully shoved him away.

At fifteen, Justin had just begun his growth spurt. He was five-ten and still growing. He hadn't filled out yet — Mark called him the string bean — but he still outweighed his brother by a good twenty

4

pounds. In a fight Mark didn't have a chance . . . but that never stopped Mark from trying.

It started out as a good-natured tussle. Mark was deliberately exaggerating his lunges for the remote. He liked imitating old slapstick comedy; the Three Stooges' films were his absolute favorites. But after a few minutes of this kind of pantomime fight, Mark paused in his attack. They were both laughing and slightly out of breath.

Mark said, "Okay, seriously now, give it to me." He held out his hand.

"No," Justin said, hiding the remote behind his back.

"Don't be a jerk. It's only fair since I got the door open."

But Justin was in the mood to torment his little brother. Mark did it often enough to him—usually when he was on the phone. It was the worst if Mark knew Justin was on the phone with Megan, his girlfriend.

"You gotta learn, little brother, that life isn't always fair."

"Come on, Justin," Mark said, getting annoyed.

Justin shook his head.

Mark went for the remote again, but this time he was serious. He grabbed for it, but Justin held it over his head, out of Mark's reach. As soon as Mark pulled down one arm, Justin transferred it to the other and held that one up—the way you would with a little kid. Finally, in frustration, Mark tried to tackle his brother, and turned their struggle into a wrestling match. Mark ended up flat on the bed with Justin sitting on his chest, his arms pinned under Justin's knees.

"You give up?" Justin asked, laughing.

"Get off, you fat freak," Mark said, still struggling to free himself.

"Say you give up."

"No way."

"You're so stubborn." Justin looked down at Mark, and he relented. He climbed off his brother, lay back down on the bed, grabbed a handful of chips, and turned his attention back to the television.

Justin knew when Mark got up, but he wasn't actually looking at him—so he didn't notice Mark open the drawer of the bedside table.

With a mouth full of chips Justin said, "See, I always win. You should write that down somewhere: Justin always wins."

"Not this time," Mark said.

Justin glanced over to see Mark standing by the bed. Mark was grinning, and he had a gun pointed at Justin's chest. Putting on a tough-guy accent Mark said, "You might want to think about changing that channel."

"You might want to put Dad's gun back or you'll be in serious trouble," Justin retorted.

Mark changed position, resting the gun on one forearm and closing one eye. "Go ahead," he said. "Make my day, punk."

"You shouldn't be playing with that thing," Justin said.

Deciding to change tactics, Mark pointed the gun at his own head. "If you don't change the channel, I'm gonna kill the kid," he said in a gruff voice.

"Be my guest," Justin replied.

For the rest of his life, Justin would never hear anything louder than the sound of the gun going off.

1

"Wake up."

The voice reached Justin through his sleep, but it wasn't a normal voice. It was a voice in his head.

"Wake up," it said again.

It wasn't like talking to himself; it wasn't his own voice he heard. It sounded deep and slightly distorted—like on television when they're trying to disguise the person and they've blacked out the face and digitally modified the voice. But it was also strangely familiar. It was like when you're having a dream and you suddenly realize you've had this dream before, though you never actually recalled it while you were awake.

"Wake up, Justin," the voice commanded.

Justin opened his eyes.

He half-expected to wake up in some strange, unfamiliar place, but there was his room, looking just like it always looked. Clothes were scattered so thick over the floor, you could barely see the carpet, and there were old glasses and plates on almost every surface. There was a time when his mother had insisted he keep his room clean, but that hadn't been the case for almost a year. Since his brother died, his mother didn't seem to care how messy his room got.

"What are you doing now?" the voice said in his head.

When Justin answered, he didn't actually speak. He didn't need to. The voice was inside his head, so he just thought his responses.

Just lying here, he said/thought. *The alarm hasn't gone off yet.*

At that moment the alarm went off, and he reached out and slapped the snooze button.

It's just gone off, he amended.

"Then get up," the voice told him.

Justin didn't want to get up. He wanted to just lie there, not thinking about anything.

"Get up," the voice commanded.

He sat up on the edge of the bed. *Okay. I'm up. What am I supposed to do now?* he asked.

"You tell me," the voice said.

So Justin did what he usually did. He got out of bed, picked a pair of jeans up off the floor, and put them on. Then he picked up a shirt. He was about to put it on, then he hesitated and gave an experimental sniff under the arm. He made a face and threw it away. Picking up another, he sniffed that, frowned, sniffed again, then shrugged and put it on.

Justin performed some version of the same ritual every morning, but today it felt different. It felt like he was going through the motions, and at the same time, he kept a kind of running commentary going in his head: *Now I'm putting on my pants. Now I'm finding a shirt. Now I'm going into the bathroom.*

When he got into the bathroom, he switched on the light and stood there a moment in front of the sink, staring at himself in the mirror. He did this every morning because his face in the mirror was always a surprise—not because it looked different, but because it looked the same. He kept expecting that because he felt so different on the inside, it would eventually have some effect—cause some sort of change—on the outside. But it was always just the same stupid face.

He brushed his teeth, washed his face, and splashed some water over his hair, smoothing it down with his hands. Then he pulled open the medicine cabinet and retrieved a bottle of vitamins from the shelf. Turning on the tap again, he filled the glass he kept by the sink. He shook a vitamin from the bottle out onto his palm, looked down at it a moment, then tossed it into his mouth and drank the glass of water.

"So you take your vitamins?" the voice asked him.

No, Justin said. *It's practice.*

Still looking at himself in the mirror, Justin opened his mouth wide, like the patients in mental hospitals when they get checked to see if they've swallowed their pills. Then he closed his mouth, stared at himself in the mirror, and spit the pill out. It bounced off the mirror and fell into the sink.

"Nice trick," the voice said. *"When do you use that?"*

You'll see, Justin said.

2

Justin was sitting at the kitchen table. His father was across from him, practically hidden behind the newspaper. His mother was bustling around the kitchen. She opened the refrigerator, got out the orange juice, poured a glass, went to a cabinet and pulled out a prescription bottle, and shook out a pill. Then she crossed to Justin and held out the OJ in one hand and the pill in the other.

Justin obediently reached out and took the pill, put it in his mouth, then reached for the glass and drank the OJ.

"Show me," his mother said.

Justin opened his mouth and showed her.

Satisfied, Justin's mother turned away, this time to fetch a bowl of cereal and a carton of milk for his breakfast.

"I thought you said your mother doesn't care about you and ignores you," the voice commented.

You think checking to see if I take my pills means she cares? Justin asked silently.

"She still gets you breakfast."

Justin looked up just as his mother carelessly tossed the bowl on the table and put down the carton of milk without even looking at him.

Before the accident his mother had been an overwhelming presence—always telling Justin to clean up his room or get his feet off the couch or do his homework or sit up straight when he ate. Despite working full-time she had always made breakfast in the morning, and they'd always had a sit-down dinner around the dining room table. Dinner was the time when Mark and Justin would be grilled about their day, their grades, their homework, their friends. Behind their mother's back they'd called it the Inquisition.

The only custom that remained from that time—Justin thought

of it as the time "before"—was that his mother still made him break-fast. But she almost never made dinner anymore. They usually ordered in and ate in front of the TV. His mother would ask him about his day—but with one eye on the television. He knew she wasn't really interested. Not in the way she had been before. And on top of that she'd stopped nagging him about cleaning his room or doing his homework or improving his grades. He never in a million years would have thought he would miss those things. But he did.

Yeah, she still gets me breakfast, Justin responded to the voice. *She also feeds the cat. And she feeds the cat first. It's like I'm not even there. She barely talks to me. She only talks to my father.*

At that moment, as if in illustration, Justin's mother turned to his father. "You've got that presentation today, don't you?" she asked.

See? Justin said bitterly. Somehow, sitting at the table with his father and mother, Justin was sure he couldn't have felt more alone—even if he were on a desert island in the middle of the Pacific Ocean. It was a piercing aching feeling. It was like being enclosed in a little personal soundproof chamber so that even if you yelled, no one around you would be able to hear.

Justin's father didn't even lower the paper to answer. "Yep," he said to Justin's mother. "It's today."

"Did you even *ask* them to reschedule?"

"No."

Justin took advantage of the distraction. Carefully, so as not to be seen, he spit the pill out into his hand and tucked it into his pocket. Then he picked up the milk and poured some into his bowl of cereal.

"*I* would have asked them to reschedule," his mother said.

Justin's father didn't respond.

"Do what you want," his mother said.

His father rustled the paper and said, "Thank you. I will."

Justin's mother turned away, and her gaze fell on Justin. She said, "What are you . . ." then trailed off.

11

Justin looked up eagerly. "What am I what?"

She shook her head. "Nothing. Never mind." Then, picking up her cup of coffee, she spoke again to Justin's father. "I've got to run. I'll meet you this afternoon."

She started toward the door, then paused and said offhandedly over her shoulder to Justin, "Will *you* be there?

Justin said uncertainly, "Um, no, I—"

His mother cut him off. "Fine," she said abruptly. "See you later, then."

"You're right. Your mother seems pretty hostile," the voice said.

Yeah, just a little, Justin replied sarcastically.

"What about your father?"

My father?

Justin looked at his father, now that they were alone together. All he could see was the newspaper held up like a barrier between them.

Justin sighed and went back to eating his cereal. He was very aware of the sound of his own chewing. That and the occasional rustle of the newspaper as his father turned the page were the only things that saved them from falling into a deep, bottomless well of silence.

Justin almost jumped when his father suddenly spoke from behind the paper.

"I don't want to hear about you getting into any trouble at school today," his father said. His voice sounded too loud in the quiet.

Justin stared at him—or rather at the wall of paper between them.

"But it's not me," he protested.

At least that got his father to lower the paper—but it was only to glare at him. "I don't want excuses, Justin. I just don't want anything happening today. Your mother couldn't take it. I don't understand why you're doing it, and I want you to stop."

12

Justin looked down at his bowl and swirled the spoon, creating a little whirlpool of cereal.

"Do you hear me?" his father demanded.

"Yes, I heard you."

"And do you promise that nothing's going to happen today?"

"Gimme a break, Dad."

"I want you to promise," his father repeated.

"Jeez. Okay, I promise."

"All right," his father said sternly. Then he raised the paper again and went back to reading.

Justin looked back down into his cereal, but he couldn't eat. He had the strangest feeling in the pit of his stomach.

"What's wrong?" the voice asked.

Justin wished that his father had been the one to ask the question instead of the voice.

It's not my fault, Justin said sadly.

"What's not?"

What's going to happen.

"And what's going to happen?"

I don't know, Justin said, suddenly confused. *I don't know. How can I know what's going to happen?*

But somehow he *did* know. The feeling was like déjà vu but stronger . . . and scarier. It told him that without a doubt something was going to happen. And it was going to be bad.

3

Justin had only a three-minute walk to the bus stop. The bus stop was down the street, just outside the guard booth. His house was in one of the private gated communities, but, as Justin's father liked to point out, it wasn't much of a community. Everyone was always carefully isolated from everyone else. They went into their garages and got into their cars and drove to work. No one worked in their own yards—they all hired gardening services to come in and cut the lawns and rake the leaves. The residents didn't walk in the neighborhood; instead they went to the gym and walked on the treadmills. And, Justin's father usually added, they hadn't even put in sidewalks—the one thing that would link one house to the next. Justin's mother always pointed out that most subdivisions didn't put in sidewalks anymore. And Justin's father always said, "Exactly my point."

There was a depressing sameness to the houses. They all had neatly manicured aprons of grass—thanks to the gardeners—with a few tastefully landscaped trees and bushes. The gate at the entrance was supposedly to keep other people out, but Justin felt trapped by it—trapped in that nice, clean, orderly version of the world. The image didn't fit his reality.

"You don't like where you live?" the voice asked.

I'd rather live in the slums, Justin said.

"Why?"

Because maybe then there would be more ugliness on the outside than on the inside. It wouldn't be such a lie.

Justin reached the front entrance. He waved at the security guard in the booth and passed through to the main road to wait for the bus.

A few minutes later the yellow school bus trundled up and squealed to a halt. The doors opened with something that Justin thought sounded like a sigh, though it was really just the old hydraulics. Justin heaved a sigh to match. Every day he thought about just turning around and walking away instead of getting on. He wondered what the bus driver would do—probably just close the doors and keep going.

But, like every other day, Justin climbed the rubber-treaded steps and faced the aisle of packed seats. His stop was almost the last before the school, so the bus was always filled. The kids were all staring at him as he started down the aisle.

At that moment the bus lurched forward, causing him to stumble. He had to grab on to a seat to keep himself from falling, and there was a burst of laughter.

Justin felt his face flush with embarrassment, and he looked around, desperate for somewhere to sit. His eyes fell on a pretty girl. She had long blond hair—silky and smooth, exactly like the hair you see in shampoo commercials—and she was sitting alone, her book bag on the slick green vinyl next to her.

She glanced up and caught him looking at her. "You wanna sit *here*?" she said, as if it were the most ridiculous thing she'd ever heard. At the same time, she put her hands on her bag as if to barricade the seat.

"No," Justin muttered, moving past her toward the back of the bus.

"That wasn't very nice of her," the voice observed.

Welcome to high school, Justin said. *The kids are all like that.*

"Not a single nice one?"

Not to me.

Justin kept walking down the aisle. Finally he found an empty seat and slid in. Wadded paper flew over his head, but the yells of the other kids faded into the background as he pressed his forehead against the glass and stared out the window. It was early October, and the leaves were just starting to change. The green was just beginning to shade to red and yellow. Fall had always been his favorite season. He knew most kids said they liked summer best, but that was usually because of summer vacation. When it came to just the season itself, there was something about the turning leaves and the freshness of the air in the morning—just cold enough to tingle inside his nose—that made him feel happy and somehow melancholy at the same time. But he didn't feel the same way about fall anymore. It had been fall when Mark died. And now, of the happy-melancholy feeling only the melancholy remained.

The bus ride was never long enough. Justin always wanted more of a buffer before arriving; too soon the bus pulled up in front of the school. It was a low sprawling building—ugly and institutional—sitting on a slight rise with more dirt than grass, and no trees to soften it.

The kids pushed and shoved, jostling to get off the bus. Justin wondered what they were in such a hurry to get to. He certainly wasn't in any rush, so he sat and waited until the last one had clumped down the steps, before he got up and walked to the front of the bus. Then, instead of clattering down like all the other kids, he paused at the top of the steps.

The bus driver must have sensed Justin's reluctance because he said suddenly, "I know how you feel, kid. I'd rather go back to prison than have to go back to high school."

Justin turned around to look at the driver. The man had only been on the job two weeks. The driver before this one had lasted less than a month—he'd quit because he couldn't take the constant heckling from the kids. The boys that usually sat in the back had moved to sit up front and had kept up an almost constant stream of taunting. A few of the girls had joined in too, telling him he was a dirty old man and that they were going to report him for looking at them funny. The driver had tried to be stern and reprimand them, but it hadn't worked. The kids were almost like a pack of wolves; they had seemed to be able to smell his fear.

When this new driver had started two weeks ago, the kids had tried the same thing with him, but he had been able to put a stop to it within thirty seconds. He'd simply given them a look and said, "Cut it out," and they'd stopped. They'd sensed instinctively that he wasn't someone they wanted to tangle with. Now Justin knew why.

"Prison?" he said. "I didn't know you could drive a school bus with a criminal record."

"Yeah, well, don't tell anyone. But personally I think it should be a requirement," he said.

Justin smiled.

"If I was back in school, you know what I'd do different?" the driver added, as Justin stood, still hesitating, on the top step.

"What?"

"I'd drop out."

4

Justin made his way down the main hallway of the school. It had a low ceiling, a thick speckled linoleum floor, and metal lockers lining the walls so every sound was magnified, turning kids' voices and the banging of locker doors into a din that was an assault on the ears. It was before the first bell, so the hall was jammed with students. On both sides there were students getting books out of their lockers, or gathered in little groups talking, and in the center, a narrow corridor of moving traffic.

Everyone seemed to be able to move easily through the crowd—except for Justin. He was jostled on all sides. A student elbowed him. Another shouldered him roughly. As he tried to get out of the way, he was bumped by someone else.

"Are they doing that on purpose?" the voice asked him.

What do you think? Justin said.

"Why would they do that?"

Because in high school there's always got to be an outsider. It's the only way the "in" people know they're "in." They need someone who's "out."

"And you're that person?"

I'm one of them. Well . . . at least now I am, Justin amended.

At that moment another student knocked into him hard enough to make him drop his bag. It was open, and a couple of books slid out onto the floor of the corridor. He stopped and bent to retrieve them. When he looked up, what he saw made him freeze.

"What is it?" the voice asked. *"What do you see?"*

Billy, Justin answered. *I see Billy.*

Billy had been his best friend—but that, like everything else in Justin's life, had changed after the accident. Justin had soon discovered that you didn't go from being best friends to being nothing, neutral. It didn't work that way. If you weren't best friends anymore, then you had to be enemies.

"So," the voice said. *"How do you feel about seeing Billy?"*

I see him every day, Justin said.

"That doesn't answer my question."

I don't feel anything. I don't care, Justin responded, with more bravado than truth. Generally Justin was okay when he saw Billy in class or in the cafeteria sitting at his regular table (the table that Justin used to sit at as well)—basically he was okay anytime he was expecting to see Billy. But in the moments when he glanced up and caught sight of Billy unexpectedly, the truth was it still felt like someone had punched him in the pit of his stomach.

Billy wasn't alone; he was flanked by his "gang": Ricky, Tim, Sam, Peter, and Evan. They were all the popular boys, the ones who ruled the school. Billy and the gang were gathered around another boy—an obvious target. Justin thought his name was Daniel. He was what adults would call a "sensitive" kid.

Billy pushed Daniel back into the lockers, saying, "Why are you such a faggot? Huh?"

Ricky—a kid that Justin had never liked, even when they were supposedly friends—chimed in, "Yeah. Fairy faggot. I heard you were looking at Billy's *ass* in the locker room."

Surprisingly Daniel managed to keep his cool. He replied calmly, "That's not true."

Ricky sneered, "I saw you. I saw you staring at his *ass*."

Daniel shrugged. "If I was, it was only 'cuz I couldn't help staring at his *ass pimples*."

Billy lunged forward at this, grabbing Daniel by the shirt and slamming him against the lockers again.

"You're dead," Billy snarled.

Justin shoveled his books back into his bag and stood up. Maybe it was the movement that drew Billy's attention, but at that moment Billy glanced away from Daniel and over at Justin.

Their eyes locked.

It was as if time stopped. Everyone else seemed magically frozen, and it felt as though he and Billy were the only two people in the world. It was like a waking dream—or rather, a waking nightmare.

"Dead," Billy said again, but his voice sounded strange. And he looked strange too. Justin peered more closely, and he saw that Billy's eyes were open but he had a greenish gray color to his skin and there was a deep gash on his forehead that was oozing blood.

Then there was the voice in Justin's head. *"Dead?"* it asked, echoing Billy's words. *"Who's dead?"*

I think . . . Billy's dead, Justin said. *He's . . . he's messed up. He's bleeding.*

"What time is it?"

Justin blinked, and just as suddenly everything was back to normal. Billy was just Billy.

I . . . made a mistake. No one's dead. It's just something Billy said. He's picking on this other kid. Justin's voice in his head was calm, but his heart was pounding.

The world had returned to normal, but Billy was still staring at him. Even though Billy had tightened his grip on Daniel's shirt, he had now switched his focus to Justin.

"What do you think you're looking at?" Billy demanded.

Justin approached reluctantly. He stopped a few feet away, glanced at Daniel, then back to Billy, and said, "You. It looks like you're having a fight with your boyfriend there."

Billy abruptly let go of Daniel's shirt and turned to face Justin.

"Don't start with me," he threatened.

"Don't make me start with you," Justin replied calmly.

"I mean it," Billy said.

"So do I."

The other boys around them followed this exchange closely. Now Ricky jumped in.

"Don't take his shit, Billy," Ricky said maliciously.

"I won't," Billy promised. He looked at Justin. "Back off." But as he said it, he took a step forward.

Justin took a corresponding step back. "Okay."

But Billy just advanced another step, saying, "I mean it." Then he reached out and shoved Justin.

Justin retaliated by taking Billy by the shirt and running him back into the wall of lockers. Billy grappled with him, and for a moment they were clinched together.

The crowd of kids in the hallway immediately began egging them on. There were catcalls and shouts, but even above the noise Justin could hear the words that Billy whispered into his ear.

He said, "You'll be sorry."

Justin let go and stumbled backward.

There was a disappointed "Aw" from the crowd. Ricky called out, "Go on. Get him, Billy."

But instead of coming after Justin, Billy turned on his friend. "Why don't you just shut up, Ricky." Then he shouldered his way through the surrounding crowd and stalked off down the hallway.

The other kids, with surreptitious glances at Justin, slowly drifted away. But when Justin finally turned to leave as well, he came face-to-face with the one person he dreaded seeing almost more than Billy.

Megan.

"Your old girlfriend," the voice said.

Justin didn't need the reminder—as if he could forget.

She was standing with her two best friends, Tina and Jenny. They were flanking her—like geese arranged in V formation, Justin thought.

"Hey, Megan," Justin said, trying for a casual tone but not quite achieving it.

Megan looked him up and down in a slow, deliberately insulting way. Then she announced, as if it were some kind of verdict, "You know, you're pathetic."

Justin shrugged to look as if he didn't care.

She looked at him a moment longer, and her lip curled in disgust.

21

Then she turned to her friends and said, "We'd better get out of here. He might decide to beat us up too."

The other two laughed. Then, as if choreographed, they all turned and flounced off down the hallway.

But as Justin watched them go, he noticed that Tina—who was shorter than the other two, a little plump, and sometimes the victim of the other girls' moods—glanced back with a sympathetic look.

5

"What are you going to do now?" the voice asked.

Justin was still standing where Megan and her friends had left him, but the hallway was almost empty now—a sure sign that the bell for class was about to ring.

Justin snorted. *What do you think?*

He knew the drill. Everyone in high school had experienced it at one time or another; your soul could get crushed, but you still had to go sit in class. That's how he felt that morning—like he'd been beaten up on the inside. But he still had to go to English lit.

In all his classes he had chosen to sit as far back as he could get. When he was lucky, he could sit for weeks without the teacher calling on him. But today was not one of his lucky days.

The radiators were clanking and the whole class drowsed in the overheated room as the teacher droned on: ". . . So to sum it up, the novel is essentially about a pedophile's affair with a twelve-year-old girl. Can anyone tell me what device Nabokov used to tell this story?"

One of the students whispered under his breath, just loud enough for the kids around him to hear, "Yeah. A fucking pencil."

There were a few snickers.

When no one volunteered, the teacher looked around the room. Finally she said, "How about you, Justin?"

Justin had been staring out the window, watching the faintest trembling of the leaves on the tree outside. The movement was so slight, he wondered if he was imagining it.

When the teacher called his name, he jerked as if poked awake.

All the other students turned to stare at him. Megan was in the class as well. He glanced over and saw her smiling at his obvious discomfort.

Justin looked down at his desk.

* * *

And that's how his morning seemed to go.

In math when the teacher asked, "Who can tell me what the root of the equation is?" and no one responded, he looked around and said, "What about . . . Justin."

There was also the struggle to stay awake. In history he put his head down, pillowed on his arms. He was just so tired. He closed his eyes—for only a second—and when he opened them again, he saw something that sent a jolt through his body. He saw his brother's face in the square pane of glass in the closed door. Mark was making faces, pulling the skin beneath his eyes down and sticking out his tongue. Then suddenly he stopped, his expression turned serious, and he said, "You're not paying attention!"

Justin blinked.

"Justin!"

Now the voice was coming from a different direction. Justin glanced away from the door and looked up at the teacher.

"You're not paying attention," the teacher said again.

Justin looked back at the door, but Mark was gone. He must have been dreaming.

"Well?" the teacher demanded.

"What was the question?" Justin asked.

"If you want to take a nap, I suggest you find someplace other than my classroom to do it," the teacher replied.

"Sorry," Justin said.

The teacher crossed her arms and said, "I mean it. I want you out."

"Yeah, okay, I'm leaving," Justin muttered.

He closed his book, tucked it under his arm, shouldered his bag, and left the room, with all the other students watching silently.

Once outside the classroom, Justin shuffled along the hallway, head down, staring at the linoleum. It was marked with the streaks from hundreds of sneakers being dragged along the floor, just as he was dragging his own now.

He heard footsteps behind him and turned around . . . to see Megan, walking down the hallway toward him.

She stopped a few feet away. She was holding a lipstick case, which Justin knew she used not for lipstick but to stash her cigarettes. When they had been together, he'd managed to persuade her to quit, but she had obviously started up again.

She stood in front of him, holding the lipstick case in one hand and tapping it against her other palm. He wondered if she was doing it on purpose, to show him that she was smoking again. Rubbing his face in it. And he figured her smoking had probably gotten worse. Before, she'd only gone to hang out in the girls' bathroom to smoke when she was with a bunch of other girls. Now it looked like she was starting to duck out of class to grab a few puffs alone.

After a moment of silence, with her standing there staring at him, Justin said mildly, "Did you want something?"

"Yeah," she said. "I want to know why you're such an asshole."

She still had the power to get to him. He literally felt a pain in his chest, as if she were stabbing him in the heart. He wondered why people felt like they had to hurt you all the time. It made him want to lash back, to try to hurt them as well.

"I don't know," he retorted. "Why do you have to be such a bitch?"

But he didn't seem to be able to get to her in the same way. She just smiled and said, "I guess you just bring out the best in me."

Then she brushed past him and disappeared into the girls' bathroom.

Justin turned away, his sneakers squeaking in the silence, and was about to continue down the hallway when his English teacher, Mrs. Elmeger, emerged from a classroom.

"What are you doing here, Justin?" she asked, looking around at the empty hall.

"I got kicked out of class," he said.

"Well, go study in the library. You can't hang around the hall-way."

Mrs. Elmeger started to walk away, but after a moment of hesitation Justin called after her.

"Mrs. Elmeger?"

She stopped and turned around again. "What is it, Justin?"

"Um. Do you smell that?" he asked.

"Smell what?"

He sniffed, as if testing the air. "I think it might be cigarette smoke coming from the girls' bathroom."

It was a serious thing to get caught smoking in school. The administration had such a problem controlling it that they'd issued a "three strikes you're out" policy: If you were caught smoking three times, you got kicked out. It didn't seem to make kids smoke any less, though, Justin had noticed—sort of like in states where they had the death penalty and the murder rate wasn't any lower.

Mrs. Elmeger eyed him suspiciously, but turned and pushed open the door to the bathroom.

Justin walked quickly down the hall. This would be Megan's second time getting caught. But maybe she'd be different and it would make her stop and think. He'd never considered smoking, because he was an athlete: soccer in the fall, swim team in the winter, and track in the summer. Though of course he had quit in the middle of soccer last year and hadn't done any of the teams since. The strange thing was that he used to love playing sports more than anything, but now he barely missed it at all.

He glanced over and saw that he was passing the glassed-in trophy cabinet. He stopped to look at the trophy the soccer team had won two years ago. He'd only been a freshman, but he had scored the winning goal in the championship game. He remembered how completely and ridiculously happy he had been. He supposed that was why adults always reminisced about being kids. They somehow forgot about all the awful stuff and just remembered that sense of being made so happy by something so small.

While musing, he had been staring into the trophy case, then suddenly he stiffened. He thought he saw something reflected in the cloudy mirrored backing of the cabinet.

"What is it?" the voice asked.

He peered closer. It looked like a figure—there seemed to be a man standing behind him, but when Justin whipped around, there was no one there.

6

"What is the difference between reality and illusion?"

The class was seated in the front rows of the auditorium. The drama teacher, Ms. King, stood in front of them, chalk in hand. Ms. King was considered one of the "cool" teachers. She was young and hip and very sarcastic (at times she bordered on downright mean), but all of the kids—even the jocks who pretended to hate theater—still tried to impress her.

She had pulled a rolling chalkboard out right in front of the first row of seats. Now she turned and wrote the words "Truth" and "Illusion" on the board.

"Anyone? Come on, what's the difference?"

Only one girl, Barbara, raised her hand and waved it wildly, as if dying to be called on.

But the teacher ignored Barbara's frantically waving hand and gazed out over the class, searching for another candidate.

"Okay," she said when no one else volunteered. "Let's start with something simpler."

Barbara lowered her hand reluctantly.

"Drama," the teacher said. "What is drama?"

Immediately Barbara's hand shot up again.

Ms. King waited a long moment, then sighed.

"Yes, Barbara?"

Barbara took a deep breath. "Drama is . . . well, it's like when someone's being dramatic. Like, you know, like—like when you accuse someone of being dramatic or . . . or like when you just *feel* things more than other people. And then they accuse you of exaggerating and they say that you're, like, being . . ."

"Dramatic?" Ms. King suggested.

"Yes. I mean—"

Ms. King cut her off before she could go on. "What do you think, class? Has Barbara captured the essence of drama?" she asked, looking around.

One of the football players, sitting slumped at the back of the class, muttered, "Friggin' theater lesbo." But he said it loud enough for everyone to hear.

And Ms. King pounced. "Jake! My goodness! Good job. Now *that* was dramatic!"

The class laughed.

Seriously now," Ms. King continued. "Before you do your scenes, I want to talk to you a little about acting and how you can tell good acting from bad acting. Let's see if you can tell the difference between when I'm really feeling something and when I'm acting."

She stood a moment considering, gazing out at the class. Then her eye lit on one of the girls sitting in the front row, and she seemed suddenly struck by something.

"You know, Sharon," she said, speaking to the girl, "I really like that sweater."

Sharon looked down at her sweater as if noticing it for the first time, obviously pleased. It wasn't often that Ms. King complimented someone.

Then the teacher looked at the girl sitting next to Sharon and said, "And your hair looks really good today, Rachel."

Rachel beamed. "Thanks, Ms. King."

Ms. King looked out at the class and asked, "So?"

There was a moment of silence. Then Sharon asked hesitantly, "So . . . what?"

"So . . . which time was I acting?" she asked.

"How can we tell? There was no difference," someone else said.

The teacher snapped her fingers. "Exactly. That's the thing. That's good acting. You can't tell the difference."

"So which time were you lying?" Jake, the football player, called out from the back.

Ms. King smiled. "Both times, actually."

There was another wave of shocked laughter, but she just continued right on. "Now let's see those scenes I asked you to prepare. You all remember this assignment, right? You were supposed to pick a scene from Shakespeare that explored the boundary between reality and illusion. Any volunteers?"

Barbara's hand shot up.

Ms. King ignored it, scanning the class for another victim.

Justin sank down in his seat. The way things were going for him today he was sure she was going to call on him. But he was lucky. Instead she said, "What about you, Megan? You did well last time with your reading from *The Glass Menagerie*."

Megan looked terrified but pleased at the same time. "Okay," she said, getting up from her seat and joining Ms. King at the front of the class.

"Which play did you choose from?"

"*A Midsummer Night's Dream*."

"Wonderful. Which part?"

"I play Titania, and it's the scene where Oberon sprinkles the fairy dust on her eyes, and she falls in love with a donkey."

Ms. King nodded approvingly. "See, class, here's a perfect example of what I was talking about. Everything is illusion— especially love. I'm sure you've all heard the old saying—that love is in the eye of the beholder, right?"

"Especially with Jake's girlfriend," Barbara called out, and she managed to get a big laugh from the class. Even Ms. King smiled.

"Right. As Barbara points out, what's attractive to one person might be repulsive to another. Not everyone sees everything the same way. That's natural. But with Titania, the problem is even bigger. She's gotten sprinkled with fairy dust. Now the trouble is, in addition to the normal differences, she's seeing the world through a distorted lens." Ms. King turned back to Megan and said, "Any time you're ready."

7

Justin crouched over, tense, staring down at the undulating reflection in the water of the swimming pool.

The crack of the starting pistol went off, and all the boys who were lined up on the blocks launched themselves into the water. Justin—whose specialty when he was on the team had always been his ability to get off the block before everyone else—was a half second late. But once he was in the pool, his arms cut through the water and his legs churned up a plume of spray. By the time he reached the far wall, he was half a body length ahead of the closest competitor.

He came up, shaking the water out of his eyes, and breathing hard. The other boys reached the wall in a staggered fashion and draped themselves, panting, over the lane dividers.

The coach walked down to the far end of the pool and stood over them. "You had a terrible start off the blocks, Justin," he said. Nothing about how well he'd swum. Nothing about the fact that he'd won anyway. The coach hadn't seemed to put it together as to why Justin might have developed a problem with the starting gun, and Justin certainly wasn't going to spell it out for him.

Justin just nodded.

"Okay, boys, out of the pool," the coach called out. "The girls' heat is up."

Justin heaved himself out of the water and padded over to the concrete bleachers where he'd left his towel. He pulled off his fabric swim cap and rubbed the towel over his hair. Then he glanced up and saw that Tina, Megan's friend, was sitting a few rows up in the bleachers, watching him. She wasn't wearing a bathing suit— she was still dressed in her jeans and sweater.

Self-consciously Justin wrapped the towel around his waist, but Tina managed to catch his eye. She smiled and said, "Hey."

"Hey," Justin replied.

There was an awkward silence. Then Justin asked, "Why aren't you swimming?"

Tina looked down at her clothes, almost as if she were surprised to find herself in regular clothes rather than in a bathing suit.

"Oh. Um. I'm allergic to chlorine," she said.

"Oh . . ."

There was another pause.

"What happens to you?" he asked.

"When?"

"When you get allergic?"

"I get, like, little blisters all over."

"Gross."

There was another awkward silence.

This time Tina spoke. "That was a nice race."

"Thanks."

"Didn't you used to be on the team?"

Justin shrugged.

Tina was about to speak, but the starting gun cracked again, cutting her off. Justin jumped nervously at the sound.

Why did they have to use guns to start races, he wondered.

"I'd better go," he said.

"See you later?" she called after him as he turned and walked away.

"Well, at least someone likes you," the voice commented wryly.

Yeah. But that just means there's got to be something wrong with her.

8

Lunchtime, Justin told the voice. *It's the worst. It makes me feel like I've got the plague or something.* He was standing on the lunch line, but there was a significant gap around him, as if no one wanted to get too close.

He shuffled forward in the line and finally got his food: a slice of pizza (not the real kind but the square kind that came frozen in big boxes with fifty slices to a box) and french fries. Then he walked with his tray down the center aisle of the cafeteria, looking for an empty table. He always hurried to the lunch room so he would get there in time to claim an empty table.

"But don't other people come and sit down with you?" the voice asked.

No, Justin said. *Never.*

But he was about to be proven wrong. He found an empty table, sat down, and proceeded to force himself to eat the food. He was about halfway through when Tim—one of Billy's gang—slid into a chair beside him.

Justin paused with the piece of pizza halfway to his mouth, then he took a bite, chewed slowly. He reached for his soda, took a sip, and without looking up he said sarcastically, "Did you come to steal my lunch money?"

"Gimme a break, Justin."

"Why should I?" Justin responded. He was trying very hard to pretend—especially to himself—that he didn't care in the least why Tim had chosen to sit down with him, or what Tim was going to say.

"Billy wants to meet," Tim said.

The pretense of not caring evaporated. Justin looked up anxiously. "Where is he?"

"No, I didn't mean now. He wants to meet later. At the back stairwell near the gym. Last period. Three thirty."

It sounded like a command. And it was one that Justin very much did not want to obey.

"You mean with all you guys standing right behind him, waiting to help him mess me up, right?"

"Yeah, right," Tim said, his turn to be sarcastic. "As if Billy would do that."

At that moment Billy himself walked by the table. He was roughly dragging another boy along by the shirt and didn't even notice Justin as they passed by just a couple of feet away.

"Why wait until three thirty?" Justin said impetuously. "We might as well get this over with right now."

"Justin, wait —," Tim started to say, but Justin ignored him. He pushed his chair back and walked toward where Billy had stopped to give the kid he had been dragging a shove in the shoulder. The kid shoved back, and Billy put him in a headlock.

"Hey," Justin said.

Billy looked around and saw Justin standing there. He let go of the kid and straightened.

"What do you want?" Billy asked.

"I heard you had something to say to me," Justin replied.

"Yeah. But later."

Ricky sidled up right behind Billy's shoulder. Like a shark smelling blood, he seemed to be able to smell a fight. "Yeah, he said *later*." But Ricky couldn't resist adding his own commentary. "Why do you have to be such a psycho?"

Justin ignored Ricky and spoke instead to Billy. "If you got something to say to me, I think you should say it." He tried to sound tough, like he wanted to face Billy down now — but this was only to cover the truth, which was that he didn't want to be alone with him later.

By this time several more of Billy's friends had gathered around, and heads had started to turn at nearby tables.

The kid Billy had been roughing up tried to break in, saying to Justin, "Let it go —"

34

But Billy pushed the kid out of the way, saying, "You stay out of it." Then he turned back to Justin, but before Billy could say anything, Ricky darted forward. He was holding a ketchup bottle in both hands, and, laughing, he squirted a stream of ketchup onto the front of Justin's shirt.

"Look at him," Ricky squealed. "Murderer. Psycho murderer. Look, he's got blood all over him."

Justin looked. There was ketchup splattered down the front of his shirt. He remembered that with Mark it had been more like a fine mist. But all over—on his face and arms and body. The ketchup was in one big glop. It wasn't at all the same, he wanted to tell them. But he didn't get a chance.

He wasn't sure what happened next. He didn't even remember looking up. Suddenly he was on the floor with Billy on top of him.

Kids flew up from their chairs and circled around. Some of them climbed up on the tables to get a better view. This was a real fight. Both Billy and Justin were pummeling away at each other. Justin was defending himself as much as he could against the rain of punches coming down at him. He hit back with all his strength. The noise of the kids around him seemed almost deafening.

Justin felt like he was trapped there for an eon, but really it was only a few minutes before one of the male teachers reached the boys and tried prying them apart, but it took two more teachers to finally separate them.

9

Justin sat outside the principal's office, sucking on his bottom lip. One of Billy's knuckles had connected and split it open. He could taste the blood. There was no other taste like it, sweet but metallic at the same time.

One wall of the principal's office was all glass, so Justin could watch the interview that was going on inside. Billy was sitting in the chair opposite the principal's desk. They had been in there talking for a while, but it looked as if they were finally winding down. As Justin watched, the principal got up, walked around the desk, sat down in the chair next to Billy, and laid a consoling hand on Billy's shoulder. Billy said something and the principal nodded his head mournfully in agreement.

"Where are you, Justin?"

Justin gave a start.

I'm outside the principal's office, Justin said. *He's getting away with it again.* He couldn't keep the emotion from his reply. It was the same story. This was what had been happening for a year now. Whenever something happened, he was the one who got blamed.

Inside the office the principal and Billy both stood up. The principal walked Billy to the door and opened it for him, squeezing his shoulder. Now, suddenly, the pantomime had words.

"You're doing just fine," Justin heard the principal say.

"Thanks, Mr. Franks."

"Okay, you can go back to class now, Billy."

Billy shot a triumphant glance at Justin before turning and exiting into the hallway.

The principal also looked over at Justin, and his expression went from sympathetic to stern.

"Justin . . . ," he said, opening the door a little wider.

Justin got up and went reluctantly through the office door.

"Take a seat," Mr. Franks said, shutting the door behind him.

Justin dropped into the chair where Billy had been sitting moments before. The principal circled around behind his desk and eased himself into his high-backed leather chair.

There was a long, heavy silence. Justin could feel the principal's eyes on him, but he refused to look up. He hunched forward and kept his eyes fixed on the laces of his sneakers.

Justin heard the principal sigh.

One of his laces, he noticed, was coming untied even though he'd done a double knot.

"Well, Justin. Here we are again." Mr. Franks paused, but Justin concentrated even harder on his laces. One of the ends was frayed—the little plastic sleeve that bound it closed on the end had come off.

"Do you have anything to say?" the principal asked.

Justin shrugged.

"We can't have this kind of thing, you know. I won't tolerate it. You can't attack other students. That's just not acceptable."

Justin looked up at that. "But he came after me!"

The principal shook his head sadly. He didn't even bother responding to Justin's objection. He simply said, "I want you to promise me you're going to leave Billy alone."

"I'm supposed to leave *him* alone?" Justin repeated, incredulous. He still couldn't quite believe that everything was getting blamed on him again.

"Yes. Are you going to leave him alone?" the principal asked.

"I guess he'd better stay out of my way," Justin said sarcastically. It was so far from the truth—which was that everywhere he went, Billy seemed to be there too. And Billy wasn't content simply to be there; he always seemed to have to get right up in Justin's face.

Justin could see he'd made a mistake in answering the principal like that. Before, Mr. Franks had looked solemn. Now he was scowling. The only thing Justin had succeeded in doing was getting him angry.

"You have an attitude problem," Mr. Franks said. "And let me tell you, I'm not going to stand for it. I've tried to make allowances for your situation, but there comes a point . . ." He stopped to take a few deep breaths, as if to calm himself. When he spoke next, he seemed to have regained control. "You know what I don't get?" he said. "You and Billy used to be *friends*."

Justin shrugged. "Things change."

"Things had *better* change," Mr. Franks said grimly. "I've tried to be patient, but I don't believe in coddling. It's time for you to shape up. Or you're out. Do you understand me?"

Justin could tell Mr. Franks meant it.

"I can't believe this," Justin said. "This is so unfair."

Mr. Franks looked at him for a moment, as if studying him. "You can think so. But, Justin, the fact is, life's not fair. Your brother and Billy's brother were the same age, weren't they?"

Why was he bringing up Billy's brother now, Justin wondered. What did he have to do with anything? But Mr. Franks was waiting for a response.

"They were best friends," Justin muttered.

"And now Billy's brother is alive and yours isn't. That's not fair, is it? But that's not Billy's fault . . ."

The principal went on talking. Justin glanced over toward the window. It looked out onto the fields behind the school. A lot of the kids had gone out there after lunch. It must have warmed up, because some of them weren't even wearing jackets. Then Justin saw Megan standing in a group of girls. As he watched, her face broke into a smile. She was laughing at something.

"Justin! Are you even listening to me? Did you hear what I said?"

"I heard," Justin lied. "Can I go now? I've got bio."

Mr. Franks looked at him a long moment. Then he said, "Yes. You can go."

Justin got up and went to the door.

"But I don't want any more trouble today," the principal called after him. "Stay away from Billy."

Justin merely nodded. He didn't bother trying to tell the principal that it might not be up to him. He was going to do his best to stay away from Billy, but there was that three thirty meeting, and he knew that Billy wouldn't have forgotten.

10

In biology Justin's teacher had gotten a rolling TV stand from the AV department, and it was positioned at the front of the room. On the screen a rabbit crouched in high grass, sniffing the air. Then it seemed to relax and started nibbling on the grass.

"A rabbit's digestive system is different from ours," the teacher announced to the class. "First of all they're herbivores. You all know what that means, right? It means they don't eat meat."

No one was really listening. They were gathered in groups around four large tables, and their eyes were fixed on the dead rabbits that were staked out on spongy mats in the center.

The teacher went on, "That means in the wild they spend a great deal of time eating poor-quality food."

One student whispered loudly to his friend, "They eat their own shit, you know." A few of the other students laughed nervously.

The teacher overheard the comment and said, "Aaron's correct. Because they eat mostly large amounts of grass and hay, they need to squeeze as much nutrition out of their food as they can. So they do eat their fecal matter."

"Gross," someone whispered, almost in awe.

"Okay now, one person from each group needs to make the first incision," the teacher instructed.

Everyone in Justin's group just stared at their rabbit.

"I'm not doing it," Aaron said.

"Me neither," his friend agreed.

"Someone had better do it or we're gonna fail," Barbara said. But for once, Justin noticed, she wasn't volunteering.

"Come on, group three," the teacher said, noticing their hesitation. "You want to get started over there. The first thing I want you to do, once you've made the incisions, is to find the cecum. I'll even give you a hint. It's part of the intestines."

No one at table three moved.

"Let's get going over there," the teacher said. "Who's going to do it?"

No reply.

"Fine, I'll do it," Justin said.

He picked up the scalpel. He hesitated a moment, then pressed the sharp steel into the rabbit's sternum and traced a line down to the belly. The skin parted as if he were pulling open a zipper.

"Remember," the teacher called out. "It's just like drawing a pair of double doors. Then you fold back the flaps of skin."

"I think I'm gonna puke," Aaron said.

Twenty minutes later the tone in the room had definitely changed.

"Now I want you to locate the kidney," the teacher instructed. "You have to move the intestines out of the way to be able to view it. Or, if you prefer, you may remove that part of the rabbit."

"Hey, it's my turn," Barbara demanded, holding out her hand for the scalpel. "I'm going to remove the intestines. I think that will be the best."

Aaron, by this time, had pulled the pins out and was moving the paws as if the rabbit were a puppet.

"No," he said in a high-pitched voice, waving the paws in pretend distress. "Please leave me my cecum."

"Sorry, Thumper," Barbara said. "You're out of luck. The cecum goes."

Justin turned away from his group and walked toward the sink. He figured he wouldn't have to be doing any more cutting now that everyone else couldn't wait to get a turn.

At the sink Justin took off his gloves and ran his hands under hot water. He washed them with soap, and then used a squirt of the Purell disinfectant; there were no paper towels, so he dried his hands on his shirt.

41

On his way back to the dissecting table, Justin passed his desk, and he noticed there was a folded piece of paper on top of his notebook. He picked it up and unfolded it.

Inside, it read, "Meet me in the back of the auditorium."

It wasn't signed, but it didn't matter. He would have recognized the handwriting anywhere.

11

Justin took a quick look around the hallway to make sure there were no teachers around before he pushed open the doors to the auditorium. He was definitely not supposed to be there—he should have been in his biology class, taking organs out of the carcass of a rabbit.

But instead he slipped into the auditorium and shut the door behind him. It was hushed and dark and a little eerie; the curtains were pulled over the big windows along the sides, and the lights were off. The rows of empty seats made it feel even bigger and emptier.

Justin made his way down the aisle to the front of the auditorium. Once there, he circled around to the side of the stage and climbed the steps. At the top he stopped for a moment and turned to look out into the cavernous space.

Standing there, he realized that this was how he felt most of the time: as if he were up on a stage, exposed—for everyone to see. Only, at the moment no one was out there watching. And Justin thought suddenly, maybe this was really what it was like; he might *feel* like he was up on a stage, but maybe the reality was that no one was watching. Maybe everyone else was up on their own stages, everyone acting for empty seats.

For some reason the thought didn't bring the relief he would have imagined. Instead it made him feel sad. And alone.

"I'm watching," the voice said to him.

That's right, you are, Justin replied, feeling strangely comforted.

He turned away from the empty seats and pushed his way through the curtains to the backstage. It was even darker there, but after a little stumbling and groping, he managed to find the prop room door.

The prop room had weak sunshine filtering in from a high window, silhouetting the racks of clothes, random pieces of furniture, a suit of armor, a bin of swords—all the bits and pieces from old productions that had been crammed into this room in case they were needed again for yet another version of *HMS Pinafore* or *The Importance of Being Earnest*.

Cautiously Justin squeezed past a rack of clothes, took four or five steps into the room, then bashed his shin against a steamer trunk with HMS stenciled on the top. He'd hit his shin hard, and he knew it was going to hurt, but the pain took a second to travel from his leg to his brain. The anticipation of pain made the actual pain, when it finally hit, that much worse. Cursing, he bent to rub his leg, then he froze there, listening. He was certain he'd heard something. Or maybe he'd just sensed her. When he swung around, he found himself facing Megan.

She was standing less than a foot away—so close he could have simply reached out his hand and touched her.

But she was the one who moved. She took a step forward so she was standing right in front of him. Then she kissed him.

For a startled moment he just stood there, feeling her lips on his, breathing in the old familiar scent. Then he kissed her back. Or he tried. But he felt fumbling, clumsy—as if he'd never kissed a girl before. At one time they'd spent hours in her basement, supposedly watching TV, but really just sitting on the sofa and kissing—they'd gone to her house because *she* didn't have a younger brother who thought it was just the funniest thing to barge in on them and then pretend he had no idea that they were there. It was what Mark had done every single time Megan had come over to Justin's house. It had driven Justin crazy—though Megan had thought it was sweet. She'd said it made her wish she had a younger brother or sister. He remembered laughing at her when she said that, and telling her she didn't know what she was talking about, and that it was *way* better to be an only child. Now he knew she had been right, and he was the one who hadn't known.

So much was different now, but being there with her in the prop room, he found at the same time that very little had changed. It all seemed so familiar. He'd forgotten how good it felt to circle his arms around her, or how soft her skin was against his cheek. He even discovered he'd missed the smoky taste of her mouth after she'd had a cigarette. When they were dating, he'd always hated that; he usually made her chew a piece of gum, which just made her mouth taste like peppermint and smoke. But now the smokiness tasted right because it tasted like her.

"Hey," Megan murmured.

"Hey," Justin said back softly.

"I know I was really awful to you."

As she spoke, he kissed her cheek. Her neck.

"Mmm," Justin said.

"And I'm really . . ."—she kissed him—". . . really . . ."—kissing him again—". . . sorry." She kissed him one more time, then added, "But you deserved it."

Suddenly Justin pulled away. He wasn't sure he'd heard her right.

"Hey, come back here," she said softly. She pulled his head back down to kiss him once more. Then she said, "You really are an asshole, you know."

This time Justin actually took a step back, so she had to let go. She stumbled back a bit, off balance from his abrupt movement.

"What is your problem?" she demanded.

"*My* problem?" he repeated.

"Yeah. You're so weird. Why can't you just be normal?"

"All right, Megan. I'll try," he said. He suddenly felt incredibly awkward. He tried to put his arms around her again, but she shoved him away, saying, "Just get off of me, okay?"

He didn't know what to do. He just stood there, staring at her.

"What are you looking at?" she said, her voice rising.

Justin backed up a step. His foot caught on the leg of a chair and he almost fell.

"You're such a jerk."

He turned to flee. Suddenly all he could think about was getting out of there.

"Asshole," she yelled.

He reached the prop room door.

"Loser."

When the door shut behind him, he couldn't hear her insults anymore. But somehow they still echoed in his head.

12

Justin bolted out of the prop room, through the auditorium, and back into the hallway. Once he was in the hallway, he finally slowed his pace, but only because he had no clear idea where he was headed. He just wanted to find someplace quiet. Someplace he could sit for a while. Someplace no one else would be.

He decided to head for the library. There were some study carrels way at the back, where almost no one ever went. He would be safe there. That's the word he thought of: safe. It was the most accurate description. He felt like he'd been under attack all day.

But before he could reach the library, he spotted the principal emerging from the staff room down the hall. He certainly didn't want to run into Mr. Franks in the hallway in the middle of a class. He looked around quickly. There was a boys' bathroom just on his right, and he ducked inside.

Thankfully the bathroom was empty. Justin crossed to the sink and turned on the tap, running his hands under the cold water. Then he pressed his hands up against his face.

"Hey," a voice said behind him.

Justin whipped around, but it was only Daniel, the undersized kid that Billy and his gang had been picking on that morning.

"You okay?" Daniel asked.

"What's it to you?" Justin asked wearily. He just wanted to be left alone. He felt like he couldn't bear a single other person speaking to him—even if it was only Daniel.

After Justin spoke, he turned away, expecting Daniel to get the message and leave.

But Daniel didn't move.

"Do you—do you have history with Ms. Hines?" Daniel asked, half-stuttering.

Justin turned back, looking at him quizzically. "Yeah."

"Did you do the paper?"

"What paper?" Justin asked.

"Oh. Guess the answer's no, then." Daniel smiled.

"Do you want something?" Justin finally said.

"Well . . . I wanted to say thanks for this morning. How you got those guys to back off. That was really cool."

Justin shrugged. "Whatever," he said, embarrassed by the thanks.

But Daniel went on. "Billy and those guys are *so* lame. I mean, I know you used to hang with them, but I don't believe in holding people responsible for past mistakes." He smiled again.

Justin eyed him, not sure how to take the last comment. "Oh yeah?" he said.

"Yeah. It's a waste of time. And you never know how much of *that* you're going to have—time I mean. It's like . . . everyone thinks they're gonna die in their bed when they're eighty." He paused, then plunged on. "But you know different. You know it can happen just like that." He snapped his fingers. "Game over."

Justin stared at Daniel for a long moment. Then he said ironically, "That is *so* deep."

But Daniel either didn't notice or, more likely, chose to ignore Justin's obvious sarcasm. "I can't even imagine what you've been through," he went on. "I tried to think about what it would be like. To see your brother die right in front of you . . ."

Justin thought about it all the time—about his brother and what had happened—but no one ever spoke to him about it. Ever. So how could Justin have known that hearing someone say it right out like that would make him feel like his foundation was suddenly crumbling. Like he was falling. Justin stared at Daniel, frozen for what seemed like forever but was probably only a few seconds. Then he spun around and slammed out of the bathroom and into the empty hallway.

Justin hurried away from the bathroom almost blindly. He passed a clock, but he didn't look up at it, so he had no idea that the minute hand had just ticked over to three thirty. He had no idea that he was headed toward the back stairwell. He had no idea he was about to show up at the exact time and place that Billy had asked him to meet.

13

Justin turned the corner—and a hand reached out to grab his arm, swinging him roughly around.

It was Billy.

"What do you want?" Justin asked. He was sure that Billy could hear the fear in his voice.

"I wanted to ask you—"

"Yeah?"

"I wanted to ask you what the hell is wrong with you."

Justin jerked his arm free. "Just leave me alone, Billy. Okay?" He started backing away. He didn't want to turn around and leave himself exposed. But as he backed away, Billy followed.

"You know what?" Billy asked.

"What?"

"I think I know."

Justin halted, and Billy did too. "What do you know?"

"I think I know what's wrong with you."

"Yeah?" Justin said nervously.

"Yeah."

Then, dropping his voice to a whisper, Billy said, "I know it was your fault."

Justin felt as if all the air had been knocked out of him. He tried to turn and run, but Billy lunged after him and grabbed him again.

"You know what I'm talking about, don't you?" Billy snarled. "I'm talking about your *brother*."

Once more, Justin tried to wrench free, but this time Billy had a better grip. Desperately, Justin shoved him with all his strength. Billy stumbled back.

Suddenly, Justin realized that the stairs were right behind Billy.

Everything seemed to happen in slow motion. As Justin

watched in horror, Billy's body tipped backward; he made a wild grab for the railing but missed, and he seemed to hover in midair, arched like he was doing a perfect backward dive off a diving board. Then gravity took effect, and he fell. And fell. And fell. It seemed to take forever, but finally he came down, his head striking the edge of the iron railing, and then one of the concrete steps.

Justin stood frozen at the top of the steps, looking down. Slowly he backed away. Then a sound pierced his ears. It sounded like it was inside his head.

The sound was the final bell.

All the doors around him opened, and the students poured out. In moments he was surrounded by other kids.

Justin turned and walked away from the stairwell quickly. His face was blank as he let himself get carried along down the hall toward the exit and the buses and home. His expression didn't change when he heard the scream; he knew someone had discovered Billy.

There was a feeling of escape when he passed through the double doors at the front of the school and went down the steps to the line of waiting buses. He found his bus, climbed the steps, took a seat toward the back, and waited. It wasn't too long before the driver turned over the engine, closed the doors, and pulled away from the curb. They were just exiting the parking lot when a police car, with lights flashing and sirens wailing, tore by into the parking lot. The bus had gotten only two blocks away before an ambulance and another police car followed.

Justin watched them go by, then turned his face away from the window.

When the bus reached Justin's stop, he climbed down the steps as if in a trance. He went by the guard in the guard shack, passing the perfect lawns and the perfect houses until he reached his own perfect lawn and perfect house. He walked up the path and used his key to open the door.

Inside, everything felt very still and quiet. Justin walked down the hallway and climbed the stairs, then paused in front of his parents' bedroom. He pushed open the door and looked at the place where the huge television used to be. His parents had moved it down into the living room, and now in place of the television was a print of Monet's water lilies.

Crossing to his mother's bureau, he opened the bottom drawer, pulled out a sweatshirt, and felt inside the pocket. He pulled out a bottle of pills. It was a prescription the doctor had given to his mother after Mark died. Justin had discovered the bottle hidden there about six months before, when he had been looking for his favorite video game, which his mother had confiscated as a punishment. It was the one and only time in the past year his mother had tried to discipline him.

Now that he had gotten what he came for, he left and went down the hall to his room. He went into the bathroom, filled a glass with water, and carried it back out with him. Sitting on the edge of the bed, he put the glass down on the bedside table. Then he opened the bottle and shook a single pill out into his palm.

He put the single pill in his mouth, took a sip of water, and swallowed. Then he took another. And another. Finally, working up his courage, he poured out a little handful and swallowed them with a gulp of water. He kept on going until the bottle was empty. Then he drank the water that was left in the glass, placed it carefully back on the bedside table, and lay down. There was something underneath his back, and he reached under and pulled out the remote control to the TV that his parents had given him after Mark died.

He reached out, flicked it on, and stared at the screen until his eyes slowly closed.

Then, through the dark, he heard a voice . . .

14

"Come on. Gimme that."

It was his brother's voice.

"Hey. Hey. Give it to me."

It was the same dream every time—or rather, it started out the same. Justin was back in his parents' room and holding the remote up in the air, keeping it away from his brother. They were past the playful stage. At this point Mark was lunging for the remote.

"Come *on*," Mark said, starting to get frustrated. He tried tackling Justin, but Justin wrestled Mark to the bed, pinning Mark's arms down under his knees.

"You give up?" Justin asked triumphantly.

"Get off me, you fat freak," Mark said, struggling.

"You give up?"

"Get off. I can't breathe."

Justin grudgingly climbed off and flopped back on the bed. He grabbed a handful of potato chips and said, "See, I always win. You should write that down somewhere: Justin always wins."

"Not this time."

There was something in his brother's tone that made Justin look up.

Mark was smiling as he pointed the gun at Justin.

"You might want to think about changing that channel," Mark said.

Justin sat up abruptly. "You shouldn't be playing with that thing. If you don't put it down in ten seconds, you'll be sorry," Justin threatened.

Mark ignored him; he was still smiling as he said, "Go ahead. Make my day, punk." Then he rested the gun on his forearm and closed one eye as if taking aim.

"I swear to God, you'll be in serious trouble if you don't knock it off."

But Mark simply changed tactics and pointed the gun at his own head. In a mock-hysterical voice he said, "If you don't change the channel, I'm going to kill the kid."

This was when the dream changed.

"I warned you," Justin said.

He lunged at Mark. He managed to get a hand on the gun . . .

But the dream always ended the same.

It ended with the soul-splintering sound of the shot.

15

"Wake up."

It was the voice again. It called to Justin from far away, pulling him out of a deep sleep.

Justin didn't want to open his eyes. He was afraid of what he would see.

"Wake up," the voice commanded.

Reluctantly he opened his eyes. He was in his own bedroom and everything looked the same. He was even dressed in his pajamas.

I had a nightmare, he said.

"I know," the voice replied. *"And then you woke up."*

At that moment the alarm went off.

No, Justin said. *I can't do this again.*

"Yes, you can," the voice said. *"And then you got up."*

No.

"And then you got up," the voice repeated.

I can't do this again, Justin insisted, but even as he said it, he found himself turning off the alarm and swinging his legs out of bed.

He sat there, waiting, but the voice was silent.

What next? he asked.

"You're the one who knows what's next. You tell me," the voice said.

So he got up, shucked his pajamas, pulled on a pair of jeans and a shirt, and went into the bathroom. He did all the same things he did every morning: brushed his teeth, washed his face, smoothed down his hair. He was about to leave when the voice said, *"Don't forget the pill trick."*

Obediently he opened the cabinet and took out the vitamins. He filled a glass of water, then tossed the pill in his mouth and drank the water. Then he opened his mouth and moved around his tongue to make sure that you couldn't see anything.

Finally he looked at himself in the mirror. It was the same old stupid face looking back at him, and he felt a wave of disgust. He spit the pill out. He spit as if he were spitting at himself, and he got it dead on. It hit his reflection right between the eyes—but this time it didn't just bounce off harmlessly. When the pill hit, there was a sharp crack. The mirror shattered as if the pill had been a bullet.

Justin stood there, staring, his image in the mirror stared back, splintered into a hundred pieces.

16

The voice spoke to him as he stood staring at his shattered reflection.

"Justin," it said. *"Justin. Time for breakfast."*

But the mirror, Justin said. *It just . . . I don't understand.*

"It's all right," the voice assured him.

Justin stared a moment longer, then, because he didn't know what else to do, he left the bathroom—careful to switch off the light—and went down the stairs and into the kitchen.

When he entered, his mother looked up and attempted a smile. "Good morning," she said brightly.

He stopped in surprise. This wasn't how it was supposed to be. She was supposed to ignore him.

When Justin just stared at his mother and didn't answer, her smile faded and she turned away, busying herself getting a glass down out of the cabinet. Then he wished he'd said something, but it was too late. He slid into a seat at the kitchen table across from his father, and a moment later his mother brought over a glass of orange juice and then silently held out a pill. Justin took the pill, put it in his mouth, and drank the orange juice while she hovered anxiously over him.

Only when she was sure he'd taken it did she turn away to get the rest of his breakfast. She returned to the table with a bowl of cereal in one hand and a carton of milk in the other. This time, instead of practically throwing the bowl down, she placed it gently on the table in front of him. As she poured the milk into the bowl, she spoke to Justin's father.

"You've got that presentation today, don't you?"

His father answered from behind the wall of newspaper.

"Yep. It's today."

"Did you think about asking them to reschedule?"

Justin was thinking about getting rid of the pill that was sitting in the back of his throat. He worked it forward with his tongue, then carefully, so as not to be seen, he spit the pill out into his hand and quickly dropped his hand to his side. He just happened to glance down at the same time, and suddenly Justin was no longer listening to the conversation between his parents—he was staring at the floor next to his chair. There was a little splash of liquid, and as he watched, another drop hit the floor. It wasn't water. It wasn't milk. It was dark red in color.

It looked like blood.

Justin looked up to the ceiling, but there wasn't any body hanging there, as would have been the case in a horror movie. He looked down again, and he saw that the blood was turning into a little puddle on the floor. Leaning over, he dipped his finger in and brought it up to look more closely.

Definitely blood. But where was it coming from?

He looked up and saw that his mother was looking at him.

"What are you . . . ?" she started to ask.

"What am I what?" he snapped, worried that she was going to see the blood as well.

"Oh . . . nothing. Never mind," his mother said. "Well, I've got to run." Then to Justin's father, "I'll meet you there this afternoon." She picked her pocketbook up off the chair and turned to leave, but then swung back around. Digging into her purse, she pulled out a piece of paper and held it out to Justin. The paper trembled slightly in her hand.

He knew what it said, even before he took it from her. At the top, in elegant calligraphy, it read, "Mark Thomas Memorial."

She said hesitantly, "Just in case you change your mind, the address is on the announcement."

Justin put the invitation down, but quickly picked it up again when he noticed that he'd left a bloody fingerprint on it.

His mother was still waiting for an answer.

He said awkwardly, "Umm . . . I don't think so."

She nodded and turned back to Justin's father. "Good luck with your presentation."

A moment later she was gone, and Justin and his father were left sitting at the table in silence. It went on so long that Justin was startled when his father spoke from behind his paper. "I don't want to hear about any trouble at school today."

All of this again? Justin thought.

"Yes. I told you it was going to be like this," the voice said.

"Well?" his father asked impatiently.

"But it's not my fault," Justin told his father.

His father lowered the paper, but this time he didn't glare. His gaze seemed more agonized than angry, and Justin had the crazy idea that his father didn't want to have this conversation any more than he did.

"I don't want excuses, Justin. I just don't want anything happening today. Your mother couldn't take it. I don't understand why you're doing it, but I want you to stop. Do you hear me?"

Justin looked down. "Okay. I heard you."

"And do you promise that nothing's going to happen today?"

Justin didn't know what to say. So he fell back on an empty evasion. "Gimme a break, Dad."

"I want you to promise," his father repeated.

There was no getting around it. "Jeez. Okay, I promise."

His father sighed as if a great weight had been lifted. "Good. I'd better get to work. Have a good day at school, okay?"

"Okay," Justin said.

As soon as his father was out the door, Justin hurried over to the sink, ran the sponge under the faucet, and returned to his chair to mop up the little pool of blood that was drying on the white tile.

Then he had to grab his bag and jacket and hurry out of the house. He was going to be late.

17

"Don't worry about it," the voice told him as he hustled to the bus stop.

Don't worry about it? Justin demanded. *It's not like it wasn't bad enough the first time around, but now I've got phantom blood dripping onto the floor of my kitchen, and you don't want me to worry about it?*

"Yes."

I'm going crazy, Justin insisted.

"You're just fine," the voice replied calmly. *"Just keep going."*

So Justin kept going. It was a good thing he had hurried, because almost as soon as he walked up to the stop, the bus rounded the corner and drew to a halt in front of him.

He wondered what would have happened if he'd missed the bus. Would everything have been different? But it was too late for that, so he climbed the steps, and the doors closed behind him.

As he walked down the aisle, he felt the eyes of all the kids—staring. Then, just like before, the bus lurched forward, causing Justin to stumble and almost fall. It was just like the last time: All the kids started laughing. But this time it sounded even louder and wilder.

His nerves were already frayed and, before he could think, he responded.

"Shut up," Justin shouted furiously.

As if on cue, they all stopped laughing. Suddenly he was surrounded by total silence. And that was worse than the laughter—much worse.

When they arrived at the school, Justin lingered at the back until all the kids had gotten off, then he walked up the aisle and paused at the top of the steps. He waited for the bus driver to speak, and sure enough, a moment later the man said, "I know how you feel, kid. I'd rather go back to prison than have to go back to high school."

After his conversation with the bus driver, Justin climbed the sloping hill to the entrance of the school. Walking down the crowded corridor, at first everything was the same as before. It was loud and crowded and kids jostled him from all sides. He was knocked this way and that—until one of the kids ran into him hard, causing Justin to drop his bag. The strange thing was that the kid seemed to rebound off him, like he'd hit some sort of invisible force field. The boy literally bounced off Justin and fell sprawling onto the floor.

Justin stared. But the boy just scrambled to his feet and hurried away, without even looking over at him.

"What is it?" the voice asked.

Strange things are happening again, Justin said. Then he added, *But I know what you're going to say. Just keep going, right?*

He bent to retrieve his bag, and when he looked up, he saw a familiar scene; Billy and his gang had surrounded Daniel.

Billy pushed Daniel back into the lockers, saying, "Why are you such a faggot? Huh?"

Ricky chimed in, "Yeah. Fairy faggot. I heard you were looking at Billy's *ass* in the locker room."

Daniel replied calmly, "That's not true."

Ricky sneered, "I saw you. I saw you staring at his *ass*."

Daniel shrugged. "If I was, it was only 'cuz I couldn't help staring at his *ass pimples*."

Billy lunged forward, grabbing Daniel by the shirt and slamming him against the lockers again.

"You're dead," Billy snarled.

It was then that Billy glanced over and saw Justin standing there, watching.

Justin braced himself, remembering that awful vision of Billy with the cut on his forehead oozing blood—the vision that had come true. But it didn't happen again.

"What do you think you're looking at?" Billy demanded.

"You," Justin admitted. "It looks like you're having a fight with your boyfriend there."

"Don't start with me," Billy told him.

"Don't make me start with you," Justin replied.

"I mean it," Billy said.

"So do I."

The other boys around them followed this exchange closely. Now Ricky jumped in.

"Don't take his shit, Billy," Ricky said.

"I won't," Billy promised. Then he reached out and shoved Justin. Justin retaliated by running Billy back into the lockers. They struggled, the kids around them yelling excitedly. Then Billy got Justin in a wrestler's clinch. His mouth was right next to Justin's ear. And he whispered into it—but he didn't say, "You'll be sorry."

This time Billy said, "I'm sorry."

Justin let go and stumbled backward in shock.

"Go on. Get him, Billy," Ricky called out.

Billy looked at Justin, and he shook his head. Then he turned on Ricky and said viciously, "Why don't you just shut up for once in your life?" and he walked away down the hall.

Justin watched him go, his heart still beating wildly—as much from Billy's words as from the physical fight. When Justin finally turned away, he wasn't prepared. He had forgotten about Megan.

He turned around and there she was.

"Hey, Megan," Justin said. Then he wished he hadn't spoken at all. He could hear the emotion in his own voice so clearly, he might as well have said, "I miss you."

She must have heard it too, because she said to him, "You know, you're pathetic."

Justin tried with absolutely everything he had to keep his face from showing that she could still get to him. But, as usual, the thing he wanted the most was the most impossible.

She said, "We'd better get out of here. He might decide to beat us up too." The words were for her friends, but as she spoke, she looked right at him. He wanted to say something—anything—to make her stop looking at him that way. But before he could think of what to say, she was gone.

18

Justin suffered through the same torture in his morning classes: He was called on in English, called on in math, and he fell asleep in history—and though he was spared visions of his brother speaking to him from the hallway, he still got kicked out of class.

After gathering his things, he hurried out of the room; he remembered that he was going to run into Megan in the hallway, and he wanted another chance to say something, though he still didn't know what.

As he walked down the hall, he worried that maybe in this version he wouldn't run into her. But as he rounded the corner, he heard the footsteps behind him. He stopped and waited, and in a moment she appeared. He saw that, again, she was playing with her lipstick case, tapping it against her palm, but suddenly he realized that she was doing it not to rub it in his face that she was smoking but because she was *nervous*. He didn't know how he hadn't noticed that before.

"That's the hardest thing in the world," the voice said.

What?

"To be able to see past your own feelings," it said. *"But that's why you didn't notice it before."*

Justin opened his mouth to speak to her. He was intending to say something nice, but somehow he found himself saying, "Did you want something?" Not only that, but to his dismay it came out in a nasty, aggressive tone. It was as if he didn't have control over what he was saying.

"Yeah," she said. "I wanted to know why you're such an asshole."

She brushed by him and disappeared into the girls' bathroom—and all he could do was watch her go.

Are you doing that? he demanded of the voice.

"Doing what?"

Making me say things I don't want to say.

"No. I don't have any control over anything," the voice assured him.

Then what are you doing?

"I'm not doing anything. I'm just here."

Justin turned around, and almost ran into Mrs. Elmeger, his English teacher.

"What are you doing here, Justin?" she demanded.

"I got kicked out of class," he said.

"Well, go study in the library. You can't hang around the hall-way."

She started to walk away, but Justin called after her.

"Mrs. Elmeger?"

She stopped and turned around. "What is it, Justin?"

"Um. Do you smell that?" he asked.

"Smell what?"

And Justin heard himself saying, "I think it might be cigarette smoke coming from the girls' bathroom."

He was horrified. Last time at least he'd been able to tell himself that Megan deserved it for the way she'd treated him. Now he knew that he was the one who had started it this time. But he'd still ratted her out. *What kind of person does that,* he wondered, half-expecting an answer from the voice.

He didn't get one.

19

Justin knew that Megan was ignoring him. She didn't look at him once during drama class while Ms. King went through her speech about drama and good acting. She didn't look at him when she got called on to do her scene. She didn't look at him until the very end of Titania's speech, when she said, "My Oberon! what visions have I seen! Methought I was enamour'd of an ass." That's when she chose to look, very pointedly, right at him.

There was a smattering of applause from the class and a couple of whistles from the boys.

"It's a sweet ass," the football player Jake called out.

"Not too bad," Ms. King said, nodding.

The class burst out laughing.

"I meant the scene," Ms. King said, but she grinned, seeing the humor in it as well.

"As a reward, I'm going to let Megan pick the next victim. Who's it going to be?"

Megan smiled wickedly. She made a big deal of scanning the rows of faces, pretending to be trying to decide, but it was no coincidence when she finally looked over at him and said, "Justin," as if in sudden discovery. "I want Justin to go next."

"Justin, where's Justin?" Ms. King said. She spotted Justin at the back, slumped down in his seat. "Okay, that's you. You're up."

"I didn't know about this," the voice said.

It's just a stupid scene, Justin replied in his head.

He got up reluctantly and made his way down the aisle to the front, where he stood awkwardly with his hands stuffed in the pockets of his jeans.

"Which play did you choose from?" Ms. King asked him.

"Um, *Macbeth* —"

"Shhh!" she said violently. "Don't you know it's bad luck to say that word in a theater?"

"What? How can it be bad luck to say—"

"Ah-ah-ah," Ms. King broke in.

Justin rolled his eyes. "I was going to ask how it can be bad luck to say the name of a play."

"Just the name of *this* play. And I don't know how it can be bad luck—it just is. Lots of strange things have happened around productions of *MacB*. Deaths, suicides, fires—you name it. You'd better be careful, Justin. One actor fell off a stage and severed his head."

"How?" someone called out from the back of the room.

"What was that?" Ms. King turned back to the class.

"How did he sever it?"

Ms. King considered for a moment. "I don't know, actually. But I do know that he wasn't a very good actor. Critics said it was the best thing for him, really—which also tells you something about critics." She turned to Justin. "So, which scene have you prepared?"

"The banquet scene."

"Does everyone know the story?" Ms. King asked the class.

Some students shook their heads.

"Okay, here's the rundown. Basically MacB stabs the king when the king is sleeping. Of course he does this because he's egged on by his wife—because according to most great works of art, a woman is always behind the real evil in the world. But that's for another class. Essentially MacB's a good guy, even if he stabs his beloved king to death. Anyway, he gets away with it, and becomes king—until his conscience starts to get to him. And then he starts to lose it. Which is why this is a good selection for our subject." She turned back to Justin. "So tell us what happens in your scene."

"Well," Justin cleared his throat. "It's right after Mac—MacB has killed the king. It's the next night and they're about to have a feast, but he won't sit down at the table because he thinks the dead king is sitting in his seat."

"Right," Ms. King agreed. Then she added, "And though MacB is the only one who sees it, it's still very real for him. What he is unable to do is to see"—she walks over to the chalkboard and underlines the words on it—"the difference between truth and illusion."

20

The boys were in the locker room, changing from their bathing suits back into their regular clothes. Justin was already changed because he'd escaped in there early, after the embarrassing end to his conversation with Tina, but a few of the boys were still in their swimsuits with their towels wrapped around their waists. They were gathered in a tight little knot looking at something on the bench.

"I bet Ms. King would say this is a great example" — Ricky made his voice high and singsong — "of the difference between *Truth* and *Illusion*."

They were looking at a *Playboy* magazine, open to the picture of the centerfold.

"They're real," Peter insisted. It was his magazine, and he'd brought it to show the others.

Another boy, Sam, snatched it up and looked at the picture more closely.

"Hey," Peter protested. "Give it back."

"They're totally fake," Sam announced, tossing the magazine back.

As it landed, it slipped off the bench and fell to the floor. Peter quickly rescued it and smoothed out the page reverently, saying, "No way. Those are real."

"Yeah, right." Sam snorted.

"Who even cares if they're real or not?" Ricky said. "Actually, it's better if they're fake. If they're real, they're all droopy and shit."

"How would *you* know?" Peter scoffed.

"Actually, he might know," Sam put in. "Have you seen his mother? She's got huge gozongas."

"Motherfucker," Ricky said, tackling Sam and crashing into the lockers as Sam laughed.

Justin was standing apart from the group, quietly gathering his books from his locker. When Ricky tackled Sam, he had to step out of the way.

"If you don't believe me, ask anyone," Sam said when Ricky finally released him. "Ask Billy, why don't you?"

Sam looked over to where Billy was standing by the bathroom stalls, deep in conversation with Tim.

"Hey, Billy," Sam called out. "Doesn't Ricky's mom have huge gozongas?"

Billy glanced around, frowning. He looked annoyed at being interrupted. "How the hell would I know?" he said.

"She was wearing that red sweater at the last game," Sam said.

That got Billy's attention. He was suddenly interested. "Oh, shit. *That* was Ricky's mom?"

"See?" Sam said, turning back to Ricky.

"Come on, Ricky. In eighteen years you *had* to have noticed," Billy said.

"That's disgusting," Ricky retorted. "She's my mom, for God's sake. That's like, well, asking Daniel if he knows how big his father's dick is."

Justin looked over to the corner of the room where Daniel was just closing his locker. Daniel had certainly heard the comment—Justin could see it in the way his shoulders tightened as if bracing for a blow—but he didn't acknowledge it.

Justin felt a stab of pity. He was usually too overwhelmed by his own problems to notice much else, but at that moment he thought about how hard Daniel's life must be. Justin was left in relative peace compared to what Daniel endured. There was barely a day that went by that Daniel didn't get followed down the hallway (boys imitating an exaggerated hip-swinging walk) or heckled in the cafeteria or ambushed on his way to the bus. And somehow Daniel weathered it all *and* seemed to be able to maintain a certain kind of dignity.

"Real heroes are usually found in unlikely places," the voice commented.

Hero? Justin said dubiously. When he thought about heroes, he thought war heroes—but really what was high school for Daniel but a kind of guerilla war? In that scenario Daniel was trapped behind enemy lines, and there was no way out. Not for years. When Justin thought about it that way, he decided that, if anything, the word "hero" was an understatement.

21

Justin was sitting alone at a table in the cafeteria, hunched over his tray, chewing methodically without really tasting the food. He glanced around the cafeteria, to see if Tim was coming, and spotted Daniel, also eating alone at a table across the room. Somehow, seeing that made him feel a little less alone.

When he turned back to his food, though, he gave a start. While he was looking the other way, Tim had somehow managed to slide into the seat on the other side of him without Justin noticing. But to his surprise Justin found that this time he wasn't scared of Tim. "Did you come to steal my lunch money?" he said.

"Gimme a break, Justin." It almost sounded as if Tim were the one who was nervous this time. "Billy wants to meet."

Justin nodded, as if he had been expecting it, which of course he had. "Where is he?"

Of course, he didn't really need to ask. Justin knew exactly where Billy was—or rather where he was about to be; he was going to be coming through the doors of the cafeteria any minute now.

"No. See, Billy wants to talk to you later," Tim explained. "The back stairwell, near the gym during last period. Like three thirty."

At that moment, right on cue, Billy passed the table, and he was roughly dragging another boy along by the shirt.

"Why wait?" Justin said. "We might as well get this over with."

He got up and started after Billy.

"Justin—," Tim called out.

Justin stopped and turned around. But when he turned, Tim suddenly shrank back. It almost looked like Tim was . . . afraid.

"What's wrong with you?" Justin demanded.

Tim stood up so abruptly that he knocked his chair over. "I was just passing along a message, okay?" he said.

"Okay. Whatever," Justin replied. He turned back to Billy, who at that moment had gotten the younger boy in a headlock. He was at it again, Justin said to himself. He wasn't going to let Billy pick on every kid who was weaker than him.

Justin strode purposefully over to Billy. "Hey," he called out.

Both Billy and the kid looked up, and Justin suddenly saw that both were laughing. And then, with a lurch of his stomach, Justin realized that the kid that Billy had in a headlock was Billy's younger brother, Zack.

"You didn't say before that it was Billy's brother," the voice commented.

I didn't? Justin replied in his head. He was confused. He thought back. How could he not have known it was Billy's brother last time?

"So you just now realized that it was his brother?" the voice asked.

Yeah, of course I just realized it, Justin said. *If I'd known, I wouldn't have had any reason to go over to get him to stop.*

But now that he'd started it, he couldn't exactly say, "Sorry. I made a mistake."

So instead he said, "You wanted to talk to me?"

"Yeah, *later*," Billy replied.

"If you have something to say to me, you can say it now." Justin thought he was speaking quietly, but when he finished, he realized that all of the nearby tables of kids had fallen abruptly and dramatically silent, as if he'd yelled or something. It was just like the bus that morning all over again.

Billy's brother, Zack, broke the silence. He took a step forward and said, "Let it go, Justin."

Billy grabbed Zack by the shirt and pulled him back, putting his own body in between them like a barricade. It was almost as if Billy thought he had to protect his brother from something, Justin thought. Then it hit him. Billy was protecting Zack from *him*.

"You stay out of it," Billy said to his brother.

"But—," Zack protested.

"I'm not letting you get messed up in this. I can handle it."

Justin was so focused on the conversation between Billy and Zack that he forgot to watch out for Ricky, who chose this moment to dart forward with the ketchup bottle. Ricky squirted it onto Justin, but this time the ketchup didn't glop out in one heavy stream. In fact, it didn't spray like ketchup at all. It was almost a geyser.

Ricky's voice came to him from far away, echoing eerily through the cafeteria.

"Murderer. He's a fucking psycho murderer. Look, he's got blood all over him."

And when Justin looked down at himself, he blinked. On his shirt the ketchup had somehow transformed itself into blood.

Blood again. First it was blood on the kitchen floor. Now it was blood on his shirt, his hands, his face. He could taste it on his lips. Like a year ago when Mark—

The room seemed to whirl, and he found himself on the floor, wrestling with Billy. He was filled with a sudden rage. He was hitting, punching, pummeling Billy with all his might.

The kids had gathered around them and were yelling, screaming, excited by the violence. Justin caught a glimpse of their faces, and it scared him. It looked as if all the kids were possessed—their eyes were open wide, their mouths stretched into gaping holes.

He stopped struggling, and Billy landed a stunning punch on his jaw, knocking his head back against the floor. As his head hit, suddenly it seemed as if the fluorescent lights got very bright. All he could see was blinding white light.

He felt Billy's weight being lifted off him, but he just lay there.

I can't see, he whispered.

"That's all right," the voice said. *"It doesn't matter."*

But I can't see, he repeated.

"You're starting to already."

And the voice was right. Even as it said the words, the blinding light started to recede. . . .

22

Justin sat outside the principal's office. Looking in through the plate-glass window, he watched the same scene play out. The principal emerged from behind the desk to sit in the chair next to Billy. Then there was the hand on the shoulder and the mournful shaking of his head. And finally they stood up and walked to the door of the office.

Then it was Justin's turn.

Justin and Billy sidled past each other, their eyes meeting briefly before sliding away.

Justin took the seat Billy had occupied just a moment before, and listened sullenly to the principal's speech.

"We can't have this kind of thing, you know," Mr. Franks was saying. "I won't tolerate it. You can't attack other students. That's just not acceptable."

"But he came after me," Justin said, though it was just for form's sake. He already knew that Mr. Franks wouldn't listen.

He was right.

"I want you to promise me you're going to leave Billy alone," the principal said.

"I'm supposed to leave *him* alone?" Justin repeated.

"Will you?" the principal asked.

"I guess he'd better stay out of my way," Justin said sarcastically.

Mr. Franks pointed his forefinger at Justin. "You have an attitude problem," he said. "And let me tell you, I'm not going to stand for it. I've tried to make allowances for your situation, but there comes a point . . . You know what I don't get?" he said. "You and Billy used to be *friends*."

Justin shrugged. "Things change."

"Things had *better* change," Mr. Franks agreed. "I've tried to be patient, but I don't believe in coddling. It's time for you to shape up. Or you're out. Do you understand me?"

"I can't believe this," Justin said. It was all so unfair—he was getting blamed for something that wasn't his fault. *He* was the victim, and he didn't understand how Mr. Franks couldn't see that.

As he sat there thinking about it, he felt the anger building and building until he thought he was going to explode. The last time he'd sat there, he'd felt some indignation, but it wasn't anything like this fury.

"This is so unfair," he muttered through clenched teeth.

"You can think so. But, Justin, the fact is, life's not fair."

How many times had he gotten the "life's not fair" speech, Justin wondered. Most of the time they said it, they had no idea. No idea at all how unfair life truly was. They didn't really want to talk about how unfair it was, what they really meant to say was, Don't complain. Don't make a fuss. Don't remind other people in case that might make them feel uncomfortable. Well, he wasn't about to go along with that. He *wanted* other people to be uncomfortable. The more uncomfortable the better—though it wasn't possible for them to be as uncomfortable as he was.

"Your brother and Billy's brother were the same age, weren't they?" the principal asked.

Last time, Justin had wondered why the principal had brought up Billy's brother. At least that was one mystery solved: The presence of Zack in the lunch room explained that.

"They were best friends," Justin said.

"And now Billy's brother is alive and yours isn't. That's not fair, is it? But that's not Billy's fault. How long has it been now? About a year, right?"

This time Justin took advantage of the opportunity to make the principal very uncomfortable. Normally he wouldn't have revealed anything he didn't have to. But this was too good to pass up.

"A year to the day," Justin said.

"It was a year ago today?" As he had expected, the principal was startled.

"You didn't mention that before," the voice observed.

After a moment the principal recovered from his surprise and asked, "Is there a memorial service?"

"Yeah. My parents are having something."

"I didn't hear . . ."

Justin shrugged. "They didn't want to make a big deal of it."

"I'm sorry, I didn't know," Mr. Franks said again.

It turned out that making Mr. Franks feel bad didn't make Justin feel any better. In fact, it was the opposite. It was like kerosene on flames. Justin had to get out of there.

"Can I go now?" Justin asked. "I've got bio."

"Yes. You can go," Mr. Franks said.

Justin stood up and started toward the door.

"I'm sorry if I was hard on you," the principal called after him.

Justin didn't even stop. He just walked out.

23

Justin was standing over the dissecting table with his group. They were all gathered around staring at the rabbit that was staked out in the middle of the table.

"Come on, group three," the teacher said, noticing their hesitation. "You want to get started over there."

No one at table three moved.

"Let's get going over there," the teacher said. "Who's going to do it?"

Still no one moved.

"Fine, I'll do it," Justin said. He picked up the scalpel, leaned over the rabbit, and pressed the blade into the skin right above the breastbone.

"Ugh," Barbara said as the skin parted.

It was like cutting a soft piece of rubber, Justin thought.

He drew the center line, then the perpendicular lines at the top and bottom so he could draw back the two flaps of skin—like double doors, the teacher said.

As he was pulling back the flaps, with Barbara ready with the pins to hold the flaps open, he was suddenly aware of a whispered conversation going on between two of the girls in his group. They had stepped a little away from the table, and up till now their voices had been too low to hear, but just at that moment their voices had risen a notch, and he could make out the words.

"It figures," he heard one girl say.

"I know," the other agreed.

"I mean, who else would do that?"

"I *know*," the other said again, with more emphasis.

"It's totally fucked up."

"Well, *he's* totally fucked up."

As he listened, he could feel the flush of embarrassment flood through him. Finally he couldn't take it anymore, and he spun around to face them. "Why don't you just say it to my face?" he demanded.

The two girls looked up in surprise, and Justin could feel the rest of the table staring at him.

"What?" one of the girls asked.

"I heard what you were saying about me," Justin said belligerently, though he was starting to feel a little unsure.

The two girls exchanged glances.

"We were talking about her *boyfriend*."

The second girl hit her friend lightly on the arm, whispering, "Don't tell him that."

"Who cares if *he* knows?" Then, under her breath but still loud enough for him to hear, she said, "Freak."

"How's it going over there, table three?" the teacher called out.

Justin turned back to the rabbit, glad to have a cover for his confusion. But just as he was about to press the scalpel into the skin once again, he saw that the rabbit's eyes were open. The eyes were bright and glistening—and alive.

Justin took a sharp breath. But when he looked around at the other students, no one else seemed to have noticed anything. So Justin simply put the scalpel down on the table very gently and said, "I think it's someone else's turn now."

He went over to the sink to wash his hands. The rabbit had been packed in formaldehyde for months, so there was no blood, but Justin didn't trust that blood wouldn't suddenly appear. It would be right in keeping with the kinds of things that had been happening.

He ran his hands under the water, as hot as he could stand it. *I'm not crazy,* he said to the voice.

But it wasn't really a statement. It was a question.

"No," the voice reassured him. *"You're not crazy."*

Justin felt comforted, but only for a moment. Then he realized the irony of the situation. The voice in his head was telling him he wasn't crazy. And how much comfort could he really take from that?

24

Justin made his way though the auditorium, Megan's note clutched in one hand. As before, he had slipped out of bio, down the hall, and into the auditorium. Now he climbed the stairs to backstage and approached the prop room door.

It would be different now, he promised himself. He'd make it different—if it was possible to change something that had already happened.

He took a deep breath and went inside. As soon as his eyes had adjusted to the dim light, he edged his way around the rack of clothes, but once again he hit his shin hard against the metal edge of the steamer trunk with HMS stenciled across the top. That didn't bode well for being able to change anything, Justin thought, stooping to rub his leg. He lifted his pant leg, and sure enough, he'd hit it hard enough to draw blood.

Always blood.

He used the fabric of his pants to blot the few drops that welled up. After the first, most intense wave of pain passed, there was a dull throbbing ache. Justin let the leg of his jeans drop back down over his sneaker. When he glanced up, he saw the shadowy outline of a person sitting in one of the old armchairs at the back, deep in the shadows. He stood there, waiting for Megan to come toward him or to speak. But she didn't move, and she didn't say a word, even though she had to be staring right at him. Then, as he stared back, he started to wonder if the silhouette wasn't too big. It seemed more the size of a man.

"Megan?" he said uncertainly.

She answered him, but her voice came from behind him.

"Justin?"

He whipped around and found her standing just a few feet

away. So who was it in the chair? When he looked back over his shoulder, it was gone. The chair was empty.

Was that you? Justin asked the voice silently.

"I don't know. It might have been."

It scared him. When it was just a voice in his head, it seemed somehow less threatening. What did the voice want? Justin could have asked, but he didn't. Because he didn't really want to know the answer.

When Justin turned back, Megan was still standing there awkwardly, looking as if she didn't quite know what to do with her hands. She looked so lost. So unsure. What had happened to the aggressive assurance of before? He waited, but nothing happened. So this time *Justin* was the one to close the distance between them. *He* was the one to bend down to kiss her.

She took a second to respond, but then, after a few seconds, her lips softened, and her arms snuck around his waist. Justin was dizzy with the feeling that he was sliding into his past, that the last year simply hadn't happened. He gave in to it; he let his mind shut down and he just floated in the feeling of kissing her.

Megan pulled back a little. "Hey," she said.

"Yeah?" Justin murmured, but then he kissed her again. He didn't want her to talk. He wanted, more than anything, to just stay with the feeling.

"Are you sorry?" Megan managed to get out between kisses.

"Sure," Justin said, not even really registering what she said.

"'Cause you were really awful to me," she said. "And I think you should say you're sorry."

At this, Justin pulled back and looked at her. He was sure he remembered Megan being the one to apologize. He was positive that *she* had admitted that she'd treated him pretty badly. But now it had gotten turned all upside down.

"Are you kidding?" he asked.

She pushed him violently away. "What is your problem?" she demanded.

"What?" he said, bewildered.

"You're so weird. Why can't you just be normal?"

He reached out for her—to try to calm her down, to get her to explain, maybe just to touch her again—but when he caught her arm, she instantly ripped it away.

"Get away from me," she spat.

He took a step back.

"Asshole," she yelled at him. "Fucking asshole."

At that, Justin turned and ran. He stumbled and almost knocked over a bin of plastic swords, then the rack of clothes. He couldn't get out of there fast enough. But even after he was out of the prop room, and the auditorium, and out in the hallway, he still thought he could hear her voice.

25

Justin was upset, even more this second time than the first. He had known what was coming—or thought he had known. The changes were starting to mount up, and something about that terrified him.

He was so rattled he didn't even remember that this was when Mr. Franks had appeared in the hallway. It gave him another nasty shock to see the principal ahead, but he was able to keep his wits about him enough to dart into the bathroom.

Still breathing hard, Justin crossed to the sink and turned on the faucet. He ran his hands under the cold water and splashed some on his face, and he had just squirted some pink soap from the dispenser onto his hands when he heard a sound behind him.

That's right, he thought. *This is when I talk to Daniel.*

But when he turned around, Daniel wasn't standing behind him. Justin looked for the source of the sound, and he saw a figure huddled against the wall, head down on his knees.

"Hey," Justin called.

There was no response.

"Hey," Justin said a little louder.

The boy looked up, and it was Daniel. His face was wet with tears.

"Are you okay?" Justin asked.

Daniel just looked at him as if he didn't understand what Justin was saying.

"Are . . . you . . . okay," Justin repeated, even more slowly.

But at that, Daniel's face twisted, and he again hid his face in his arms.

Justin stared at him for a moment, but Daniel didn't look up, so Justin turned back to the sink to wash off the soap. But as he held out his hands underneath the water, he saw that instead of pink soap they were smeared with blood.

For a second he couldn't breathe.

He fled from the bathroom and burst out into the hallway, wiping his hands desperately on his shirt.

I want it to stop. I want you to stop it now, Justin demanded, walking quickly down the hall.

"I can't do that," the voice replied.

Why not?

"It's time," the voice said gently.

Justin passed a clock and glanced up. Its hands showed that it was three thirty.

Justin stopped abruptly.

I'm not going, he said.

"You can't change it now," the voice told him.

Yes I can, Justin insisted. *If I just stand here and don't move . . .*

But he blinked, and suddenly he found he was standing in the corridor by the back staircase.

He whipped around to check behind him, but there was no one there. He still had time to get away. He turned back—and ran smack into Billy.

"Justin . . . ," Billy said.

Justin spun around to flee in the other direction, but Billy reached out and grabbed his arm.

"What do you want?" Justin demanded, anxious to get away.

"I wanted to ask you . . ."

Justin stared at Billy. Billy's mouth was moving, but it was as if Justin were watching a movie and the sound had cut out.

"What is he saying?" the voice asked.

Justin didn't answer. Instead he found himself grabbing Billy and saying desperately, "Just leave me alone, Billy. Okay?"

Billy laughed. "You want *me* to leave *you* alone?" Then he laughed again, but this time it had a strange, hollow sound. It raised goose bumps on Justin's arms.

"Shut up," Justin yelled, shaking Billy hard.

Billy stopped laughing. "You know what?" he said, suddenly very serious.

Justin let go of Billy and took a step back. "What?" he asked.

"I think I know."

Justin started backing away, but Billy matched him step for step.

"What do you know?"

"I know what's wrong," Billy said.

"Yeah?"

"Yeah," Billy replied. "I know it was your fault."

Justin spun away, but Billy lunged after him and grabbed him. As Justin tried to wrench himself free, he shoved Billy backward.

Billy teetered for a moment at the edge of the stairs. Justin leapt for him, but as he clutched for Billy's shirt, instead of grabbing it he actually tipped the delicate balance and sent Billy tumbling back.

Into thin air.

Billy's body made the same graceful arc through space, and then his head struck the iron railing with the same solid *thwack*.

Justin stood there, gasping. He felt like he was choking on air.

At the shrill clamor of the bell he turned and ran. The students poured into the corridor from the classrooms, and he was soon surrounded by other kids, all talking and laughing, happy that it was the end of the day.

Justin pushed through them, oblivious. His body was on autopilot, and his face had been chipped from a block of ice. But there must have been something strange about his expression, because a lot of the students stopped to stare at him as he went by. Until the air of the hallway was pierced by a scream.

Everyone else seemed to freeze in place, except for Justin. He kept right on walking. He walked down the hallway, walked out through the front doors, walked down the hill to his bus. As he climbed the steps and went to take a seat, the bus driver turned and stared at him, just as the students had.

"Hey, kid, are you okay?" the driver called after him as he continued down the aisle.

Justin stopped and glanced around. He didn't know why the bus driver would be asking him that. The driver couldn't know anything. Could he?

"Yeah," Justin said. "I'm fine." Then he hurried on and took a seat toward the back.

Then the doors closed, and as the bus pulled out of the parking lot, the sirens sounded faintly in the distance.

26

When Justin let himself into his house, the stillness seemed bottomless. It was like time had stopped. It was like he was the only one left in the whole world.

He dropped his bag in the hallway and wandered through the empty living room to the stairs. He climbed slowly, resting his palm on the banister, just brushing the wood. When he reached the second floor, he started down the hall, running his fingertips along the wall. He let his fingers ride over the molding and the door of the bathroom, then of his room, but when he reached the third door, he paused. He dropped his hand to the doorknob, and let it rest there a moment. Then he slowly drew it back again—and continued down the hallway. Strangely, he found it hard to walk a straight line without his fingers brushing the wall. But it was only a few more steps to his parents' bedroom. He went in, this time without hesitation, and crossed straight to the bureau, opening the bottom drawer and retrieving the bottle of pills. Then he turned and retraced his steps back down the hall to the bathroom, where he filled a glass of water. Then he looked into the mirror. The glass was still shattered, and he stared at his fragmented reflection.

"I want this to be over," he said quietly. "I just want this to be over."

He stared a moment longer, then abruptly turned away and retreated into his bedroom.

Sitting on the edge of the bed, he started with one pill. Then a second. And a third. Then, as he worked up his courage, he took them in small handfuls. He kept going—automatically, systematically—until the bottle was empty. Then he lay back down on the bed. As he did, he accidentally pressed the power button on the remote, which was lying, half-hidden, under a fold of the covers, and the TV flicked on. He picked up the remote to turn the TV off, but on second thought he just lowered the sound. Then he lay back down on the bed.

He closed his eyes. . . .

When he opened them again, Mark was standing on the other side of the bed, with the gun trained on Justin's chest.

Justin sat up so quickly that he felt dizzy.

"Give that to me," Justin said urgently, reaching his hand out for the gun.

"Yeah, like you gave me the remote," Mark scoffed.

"I'm serious, Mark," Justin said.

"'I'm serious, Mark,'" Mark mimicked.

Justin lunged toward him.

"Hey," Mark protested, struggling, but Justin grabbed Mark's wrist in one hand, and wrenched the gun free with the other.

"See?" Justin said, triumphantly holding up the prize. "What did I say? I always win. You should write it down."

Mark just scowled at him.

"And don't touch this again," Justin said. "This isn't something you should be playing with. And don't you know you should never, ever point a gun at anyone? How would you like it if I pointed it at you?"

"I wouldn't care," Mark retorted.

"Oh, you don't think so? I bet you would."

And Justin raised the gun.

27

"Wake up."

This time Justin didn't obey the voice. Instead of opening his eyes he squeezed them shut even tighter.

No, he said. *Not again.*

"Once more," the voice insisted.

Even with his eyes squeezed shut, a tear managed to seep out from beneath his lashes. *I can't do it again,* he whispered.

"This is the last time," the voice promised.

Another tear leaked out, and Justin mutely shook his head.

"WAKE UP!" the voice commanded.

Justin's eyes snapped open. It wasn't even a choice; it was involuntary, like when the doctor hit your knee with the rubber mallet and your foot jerked up. That's how it felt when the voice spoke like that.

He lay there, waiting for the voice to speak again. But it didn't, and he discovered that the silence was even worse — the longer it stretched, the more tense Justin became.

Finally he broke.

I'm getting up, he said breathlessly. *I'm getting dressed. I'm going into the bathroom.* He reported his actions without further protest.

Once in the bathroom he squeezed toothpaste onto the toothbrush, ran the bristles under the faucet, and went at his teeth like he was sawing wood. He spit and laid the brush down on the side of the sink, not even bothering to rinse it. Then he splashed water on his face and, still bent over the sink, ran both hands through his hair to smooth it down — all without looking in the mirror. And finally he filled the water glass. He took the vitamin, put it in his mouth, and swallowed the water.

Only then did he look up into the mirror. He opened his mouth, making sure he couldn't see the pill. Then he spit it out. It hit the glass and bounced harmlessly into the sink; the mirror remained intact.

Now that he was looking in the mirror, Justin found himself staring at his reflection. The eyes in the mirror narrowed, the face twisted, and the expression was so ugly and bitter he barely recognized it. But a second later he did—because that's when he felt the emotion that he saw reflected in the mirror rising inside him like a tidal wave. It flooded over him, swamping him. He felt like he was drowning in it. It was hatred. And loathing. And disgust. And it was all for that stupid face in the mirror.

And then his fist was in the air, and he was smashing it against the glass, splintering his reflection into a hundred little fragments. He let his hand drop back to his side, staring at the spiderweb of lines that now decorated the mirror. It wasn't any magic that had shattered the glass; it wasn't a pill with the force of a bullet. He wished it had been. Somehow, he felt like that had actually been less frightening.

28

"Good morning," his mother said as Justin entered the kitchen.

"What's good about it?" Justin heard himself snapping.

His mother turned quickly away—under the guise of getting the orange juice out of the refrigerator—but she didn't turn away quickly enough, because Justin caught a glimpse of the look on her face. When he had come in, she'd been smiling, but as soon as he spoke, her face crumpled, as if it were only through an enormous effort of will that she kept from bursting into tears.

When Justin took a seat at the table across from his father, he saw the newspaper tremble in his father's hands.

His mother busied herself getting out a glass, pouring out his orange juice, getting out the prescription bottle, and shaking out a pill. When she turned to Justin again, she had managed to regain control over her face. Her expression when she handed him the orange juice and held the pill out on her palm, was smooth and serene.

Justin took the pill. He felt guilty about what he'd said, but he couldn't seem to find the words to apologize. That made him feel even worse, and somehow it all got turned around inside him, and he found himself getting angry at her for making him feel bad. And before he knew it, he was snapping at her again.

"What, are you going to stand over me like a jailor while I take it?" he demanded.

She turned away again silently, this time to get the bowl and milk for his cereal, but Justin noticed that *both* his parents—his mother while she opened the refrigerator and his father by turning the page of the paper—managed to watch covertly as he put the pill in his mouth and drank his orange juice.

His mother returned to the table with a bowl in one hand, a

carton of milk in the other, and the box of Cap'n Crunch under her arm. She never used to let them eat sugar cereals. It was always cornflakes or Grape-Nuts or something equally disgusting and healthy. He and Mark had barely bothered to campaign for anything else. They'd known that they had no chance of winning. But after Mark died, some awful, calculating part of him had known it was an opportunity to get whatever he asked for. So he had asked. His mother tried to put up a fight. She said, "You know I don't let you eat that junk. It's not healthy."

"So what?" Justin shot back. "It didn't matter for Mark. He could have had Cap'n Crunch every day of his life, and it wouldn't have made a bit of difference—except that he might have been a little happier." Even before the words left his mouth, Justin knew he shouldn't have said it. But it worked; the next day his mother brought home Cap'n Crunch from the store. The thing was, when his mother set the cereal on the table in front of him that first day, instead of being happy about getting what he wanted, Justin had felt like he'd been punched in the gut. That's when he'd realized that what he'd *really* wanted was for his mother to refuse to buy him Cap'n Crunch—just like she'd always refused—because then he would have had proof that what had happened with Mark hadn't changed everything.

After the cereal he tried again, with bigger things. He asked for a TV in his room. And then for a PlayStation. And then for a new computer. He was trying to force her to revert back to how she'd been before, but instead, each time his mother put up even less of a fight. Finally Justin had to switch tactics. He started "talking back," as his mother called it. But Justin knew it was more than just the normal teenage rebellion. He went past the boundaries of normal obnoxiousness. In fact, he tried to be as hurtful as possible. He just wanted to get a response out of her. But it didn't work. After a few brief battles his mother started ignoring his behavior. In fact, the ruder Justin got, the nicer she became. He knew it didn't mean anything. Like her getting his breakfast now didn't mean anything.

She doesn't care, Justin told the voice. *She just doesn't want to have to deal with me.*

But even as he said it, he could feel rather than see the covert glance his mother stole to check on him. And he could picture the worried expression that creased her face. And he realized that nothing he'd said was true.

"No," the voice agreed. *"It isn't true."*

Meanwhile, his mother was speaking to his father.

"You've got that presentation today, don't you?" she asked.

"Yep. It's today."

"And you didn't want to ask them to reschedule?"

This time as Justin listened, it didn't seem like they were ignoring him. It seemed, in fact, that they were just straining to make conversation to try to keep the appearance of normality in the face of his sullen silence.

But he still had to get the pill out of his mouth. When he was sure neither of his parents was looking, he brought his hand up to his mouth as if to scratch his nose, and he surreptitiously palmed the pill.

Something splashed onto the table. He moved his hand, and the next drop fell in his cereal, red immediately turning to pale pink as it dispersed in the milk. He quickly dropped his hand to his side, and the next drop fell on the tile next to his chair.

Blood.

He must have cut his hand hitting the mirror, he realized. How could he not have noticed?

He glanced down, trying not to call attention to his movements. It wasn't a bad cut, he saw with relief. It was the action of making a fist around the pill that had squeezed the blood from the cut. He would have to get a few Band-Aids after his parents left and before he went to catch the bus. He could only hope that until then he would be able to hide it from them.

"What are you thinking of . . ."

Justin glanced up sharply when he realized his mother was speaking to him. His look made her falter.

"What am I thinking of what?"

Now all he wanted was for her to ignore him. It was funny: He wanted her attention, but at the same time he didn't want it. If she saw his hand, he knew she would have a fit. She would demand to know how it had happened, and he would have to tell her about what he'd done to the mirror. He knew instinctively how upset she would be. Then it would turn into this big deal. She would keep after him about why—why had he done it? And he would pretend to be angry at her for asking because the truth was, he *couldn't* answer. He didn't know why. And he couldn't possibly tell her how scary that was.

"Why couldn't you tell her that?" the voice asked.

Because she's already scared, Justin said. *I'm not sure she can handle any more.*

"But can you handle it?"

Justin didn't answer the voice. He didn't have an answer. So he answered his mother instead—it was easier.

"What am I what?" he said again, a little more gently, but that seemed to upset her even more than his abruptness.

"Nothing," she said, turning away quickly, and he knew she was on the verge of tears. "Well, I've got to run," she said. Her voice had that ring of false brightness, and she made herself very busy gathering up her purse and keys. She started toward the door, then she hesitated and turned back.

"You didn't change your mind about coming today, did you?" she asked him.

"No," he said.

"Okay." But still she hovered a moment. Then she said quickly, "Just in case you change your mind, here's the address." She put a small invitation on the table that read, "Memorial for Mark Thomas." Then, somewhat flustered, she hurried out the door.

Justin and his father were left alone.

There was a kind of vacuum left by his mother's departure. They sat in silence, but Justin, with his strangely heightened senses, knew that in the silence they were both intensely aware of the other. It was a silence filled with anticipation, like the breath before speech.

Finally his father lowered the paper. He spoke in a hearty, joking voice that was as false as Justin's mother's brightness.

"So, do you think you can manage to stay out of trouble at school today?" he asked, with a smile tacked on to soften the words.

"I told you before, it's not me," Justin retorted.

"I know." His father held his palms out, in a kind of apology. "I understand that. I know it's not you. But could you maybe just try to avoid him? Just for today?"

"Avoid him?" Justin's voice climbed. "How am I supposed to do that? He's in half of my classes."

"Well, just do your best. That's all I'm asking. It's just that if something happened today . . . I don't think your mother could take it."

"I don't know why you're assuming that something is going to happen," Justin said sullenly.

"Just promise me."

Justin felt an unreasoning anger. Why couldn't his father just leave him alone?

"I want you to promise," his father repeated, almost pleading.

He saw that his father wouldn't leave off until he got his stupid promise. But you couldn't force a promise out of someone, Justin thought. And if you tried, you deserved whatever you got.

"Okay. I promise," Justin said, taking an almost perverse satisfaction out of the knowledge that the promise wasn't going to do his father a bit of good.

29

Justin almost missed the bus. When his father finally left for work, Justin had to clean the spots of blood on the floor and put some peroxide and Band-Aids on his hand. He almost forgot his bag, and had to go back for it. By the time he jogged, huffing, up to the stop, the bus was already pulling up.

The doors opened, and Justin climbed the treaded steps. Pausing to check for empty seats, he noticed that this time the whole bus wasn't staring at him like they had before. Sure, there were a few kids who looked. But all of them, the moment he caught their eye, looked quickly away.

Justin started walking down the aisle. When the bus lurched forward and he stumbled—for the third time—he thought ironically how this seemed to disprove that old saying that you could learn from your mistakes. That didn't appear to be part of the rules of this strange day. He wasn't actually able to change or avoid anything— yet nothing was exactly the same twice.

This time it wasn't the embarrassing near-crash of before; it was only a little misstep. And instead of the whole bus breaking into shrieks of laughter, it was only one kid who started to giggle, a nervous kind of laugh.

Justin glared at the skinny, undersized freshman who was the source of the noise, and the kid cut off that laugh so fast you might have thought Justin had hit some sort of mute button. The kid looked positively scared, Justin realized with satisfaction. But Justin didn't get to enjoy the feeling for long.

Walking down the aisle, looking for an empty seat, Justin paused next to a girl sitting alone. He recognized her—and then he didn't. She had the same long, silky blond hair. But in the other versions she had been pretty. Now as he looked, he could see that she had braces, and pimples dotting her cheeks and forehead.

"You can sit here if you want," she said quickly, as soon as she felt his gaze on her, and she reached over to move her bag out of the way. In her reaction Justin sensed the same tinge of fear he had seen in the other boy's face; but the fact that a girl was scared of him didn't make him feel powerful. It made him feel like a monster. And, somehow, it made him act like one too. He heard himself saying viciously, "I wouldn't sit there if you paid me, pizza face."

The kids near enough to overhear started to laugh.

The girl turned her face away quickly, trying to pretend like she didn't care, but Justin knew better—because he'd spent so much time feeling just the same way. He knew all about knowing that you weren't quite "right," that you didn't fit in, that everyone was staring and pointing and laughing. And now, he thought bitterly, here he was, doing it to someone else.

Justin hurried past the girl and slid into an empty seat at the back of the bus, but he couldn't get it out of his mind. He wondered if it was like a kind of chain: You felt this way, and that made you turn and attack someone else and pass along the feeling, and they did the same, and on and on and on. It was like some sort of virus— one that you spread intentionally. He looked up, and out of the window he saw the building that was like a petri dish for the virus.

They had arrived at school.

30

The bus pulled up, and Justin waited until all the other kids had gotten off before reluctantly getting up and shuffling to the front of the bus. He paused at the top of the steps.

The bus driver said, "I know how you feel, kid. I'd rather go back to prison than have to go back to high school."

"I didn't know you could drive a school bus with a criminal record," Justin said.

"Yeah, well, don't tell anyone. But personally *I* think it should be a requirement," the bus driver replied.

Justin smiled.

"If I had to go back to high school, you know what I'd do different?" the driver added, as Justin stood, still hesitating on the top step.

"What?"

The driver smiled. "I'd drop out."

The conversation was comfortingly, reassuringly the same as it had been twice before. It was like a pillar of stability, when the rest of the foundation of the day seemed to be shifting under him—until Justin stopped to wonder why, out of all the students, the bus driver had chosen to confide in him. The man wasn't exactly the kind to comfort the underdog. You could tell that when he was in school he'd been more the type to beat up the underdog. That was part of the reason he'd gotten such immediate respect from the kids. So why had the man chosen him?

With that unanswered question still in his mind, Justin climbed the hill to the school with a sense of foreboding.

The hallway was packed with kids, but as Justin walked down the corridor, most of them tried their best to get out of his way. If they weren't able to, Justin found himself roughly shouldering his way through. Before, he had been the one who was pushed and shoved, not the one who was doing the pushing and shoving. Hadn't he?

At that moment a younger boy stumbled, bumping into him. But it wasn't like before. This time it was completely unintentional. The boy had been walking with a pack of friends, and one of them had mischievously knocked him into Justin's path. But even having seen that, it didn't stop Justin from giving the boy a shove that sent him flying. The boy dropped his bag, and books skidded out across the floor of the hallway.

Justin stopped to watch the boy scramble to gather up his books. Hadn't those been his own books before, scattered across the hallway?

The other students, hurrying along, stepped on the books, and some even kicked the books on purpose as the boy tried to gather them together. The boy's friends didn't even try to help. They just stood there, cackling—doubled up and holding their stomachs—to emphasize how funny they found it all. When Justin looked, he could see that the boy was almost in tears.

He turned away, only to be confronted by another, more familiar scene: Billy was shoving Daniel back into the lockers, saying, "Why are you such a faggot? Huh?"

Ricky put in his line, "Yeah. Fairy faggot. I heard you were looking at Billy's *ass* in the locker room."

Unlike the boy scrambling to get his books, Daniel seemed unfazed by the situation. "That's not true," he replied.

Ricky sneered, "I saw you. I saw you staring at his *ass*."

Daniel shrugged. "If I was, it was only 'cuz I couldn't help staring at his *ass pimples*."

Billy lunged forward at this, grabbing Daniel by the shirt and slamming him against the lockers.

"You're dead," Billy said.

As Justin watched, the simmering anger he'd been feeling all morning boiled suddenly into rage.

"No, he's not," Justin called out from where he stood.

His voice was loud enough that everyone in the hallway turned around to look at him.

"You're the one who's dead," Justin said. He strode over, stopping a couple of feet away. "It looks like you're having a fight with your boyfriend," he sneered, looking at Billy.

Billy quickly dropped his hands from Daniel's shirt.

"Don't start with me, Justin," he said, but it sounded more like a plea than a warning.

"So *I'm* starting with *you*? What are *you* doing?" he said, looking at Billy, then pointedly at Daniel.

"Don't take his shit, Billy," Ricky cried out.

Billy ignored Ricky and spoke quietly to Justin. "This doesn't have anything to do with you. So just back off, okay?"

"Yeah, sure," Justin said, but instead he took a step closer.

"I mean it," Billy said.

"I'm sure you do," Justin said, but his tone was mocking, sarcastic. And this time he took two steps forward, so he was standing right up in Billy's face.

Billy really had no choice. He gave Justin a rather tentative shove, but that was all that Justin needed—he retaliated with a body tackle, and they crashed back into the lockers. There was a hollow boom as the metal reverberated with the impact of their weight.

Justin was only vaguely aware of the shouts from the other kids as he and Billy grappled for a hold. Billy's mouth was right by his ear, and Justin could hear him breathing hard. And then he spoke. He said, "Justin, don't. Listen, I'm sorry. Okay?"

No one except for Justin heard Billy's whispered words. Justin wished he hadn't either. He wished he were back in the first version of the day, when the whispered words had been a threat rather than an apology. The apology ruined the pureness of his rage. Before Billy spoke, Justin had had the feeling of getting carried along on the crest of a powerful wave, a wave of righteous anger. But the apology had sent the wave crashing down—right on top of him.

Even though Justin had the advantage, at Billy's words, he let go and stumbled backward.

"Go on. Get him, Billy," Ricky called out, seeing this as an opening. "Why don't you get him?" Ricky prodded as Justin and Billy stood there staring at each other.

"Shut the fuck up, Ricky," Billy said. Then he turned and stalked off.

Justin turned to escape as well, but of course, instead he came face-to-face with Megan.

She just stood there, staring at him.

"What the hell do *you* want?" he demanded after a moment of heavy silence.

A hurt look flashed across her face. It was gone in another instant, so fast it was like a single frame in a film. But with his seemingly heightened perceptions, Justin caught it.

"You know, you're pathetic," she said. Then, turning to her friends who hovered behind her, she said, "Let's get out of here before he decides to beat us up too."

31

Justin sat in the back of the room in English. The whole class seemed to drowse as Mrs. Elmeger droned on.

". . . essentially about a pedophile's affair with a twelve-year-old girl. Can anyone tell me what device Nabokov used to tell this story?"

A boy in the back near Justin whispered under his breath, "Yeah, a fucking pencil."

A few of the kids around them laughed, drawing the teacher's attention to the back of the room.

"Justin," she called out. "How about you? Can you tell us what device the author used?"

Justin looked up.

Everyone in the room turned to stare at him. Justin saw Megan smirking at him.

He looked down again and mumbled something.

"What's that you said, Justin?" Mrs. Elmeger prompted. "We couldn't hear you."

He started to speak, but his voice was hoarse, so he had to clear his throat.

Mrs. Elmeger crossed her arms, as if to say, "Okay, let's have it."

"Unreliable narrator," Justin said. "That's the device Nabokov used."

There was a moment of shocked silence. Mrs. Elmeger's arms dropped back to her sides.

"That's right," she said. "Justin is absolutely correct."

Justin wasn't quite as lucky in his next few classes. He didn't know the answer when he was called on in math, and he got kicked out again for falling asleep in history. He wondered if that meant some-thing—that he couldn't seem to stay awake in history. History was something he wanted to forget. Something that caused him to retreat into the oblivion of sleep.

When the teacher ordered him out of the room, he gathered together his books and shouldered his bag. He knew what was com-ing. He knew exactly when Megan was going to appear, but when she rounded the corner, this time he tried to just keep walking. The idea of talking to her triggered a kind of panic.

But Megan stopped and said, "Hey."

He couldn't quite bring himself to simply ignore her, so he stopped as well and said, "Hey."

There was a moment of silence, and Justin looked down at his feet.

"I can't believe you knew that answer in English earlier," she said.

A part of him knew that she was trying to give him a compli-ment, but it was easier to pretend it was an insult.

"Why is that so surprising? You think I'm stupid or some-thing?"

Megan stared at him a moment, then she was the one to look down. She started playing nervously with something in her hand—her lipstick case.

"N-No," she half-stuttered. "I mean . . . *I* didn't know it, is all."

"Well, I guess some of us are smarter than others," Justin said. It was as if someone else were controlling the words that came out of his mouth.

"Why do you have to be such an asshole?" she demanded.

"Dunno. I guess you just bring out the best in me."

Finally she'd had enough. She rushed past him and escaped into the girls' bathroom.

Justin turned away and started walking down the empty hall. That's when he ran into Mrs. Elmeger. It was clear that he was the one who had been awful to Megan, but somehow it didn't make a difference. He wanted to hurt her, and so he found himself saying, "Do you smell that? It smells like smoke."

"I don't smell anything," Mrs. Elmeger said, sniffing.

"I definitely smell it," Justin said. "And I think it's coming from the girls' bathroom."

And he felt an awful sense of satisfaction as he watched Mrs. Elmeger push open the bathroom door.

32

Justin tried to breathe normally, but it was hard, standing on the stage with the whole class looking at him. Ms. King was standing next to him, with his copy of Macbeth, so she could read the other parts and see where he'd edited the scene.

He tried to draw as much air into his lungs as possible, and recited his first line.

"The table's full," he said. His voice was husky with fear, but it was okay because it worked with the part.

Ms. King squinted at the text, and read out the servant's part in a high, mocking parody of subservience, "Here is a place reserved, sir."

The class laughed at her squeaky servant's voice, and that relaxed Justin a bit, since he felt like the attention had shifted away from him.

"Where?" he asked, and glanced around as if looking for the place.

"Here, my good lord. What is't that moves your highness? Gentlemen, rise: his highness is not well."

Ms. King changed to a low, throaty tone for the part of Lady Macbeth. She made as if she were addressing the class sitting in the auditorium seats. "Sit, worthy friends: my lord is often thus, and hath been from his youth: pray you, keep seat; feed, and regard him not."

Then she turned to Justin and in a harsh whisper said, "Are you a man?"

She said it with such intensity that he felt the sting of her contempt, even though he knew she was just saying the lines. How must Macbeth have felt, to have his wife speaking to him like that? Especially after what he had done. Justin threw his head back. "Ay, and a bold one, that dare look on that which might appal the devil," he retorted.

"O proper stuff! This is the very painting of your fear: When all's done, you look but on a stool." And Ms. King gestured toward the empty chair they had set in the middle of the stage.

"Prithee, see there! behold!" Justin raised his arm and pointed at the seat and the ghost that Macbeth could see, but who was invisible to everyone else. He meant to do it majestically, but he felt his finger trembling. "Look! lo!"

He remembered picking this speech, thinking that it would be easy for him. It would barely count as acting. For a while it happened to him almost every day. Mark came back in dreams that were so real, Justin could barely tell they were dreams. He would see his brother in the most ordinary situations, doing what Mark used to do, clowning around, watching TV, being a pest. Sometimes he was just his old self. But sometimes Justin saw him as he'd seen him last—with half his head blown away.

When Justin spoke next, he directed his words to the ghost in the chair. "How say you? Why, what care I? If thou canst nod, speak too. If charnel-houses and our graves must send those that we bury back—"

"What, quite unmann'd in folly?" Ms. King interjected.

But Ms. King had lost the class's attention. All eyes were on Justin now. His voice dropped to a terrible whisper.

"The times have been, that, when the brains were out, the man would die, and there an end; but now they rise again." The harsh whisper died out and Justin stood on stage, staring at the empty chair.

For several seconds he stood rooted to the spot, and he stared so intensely at the empty chair, most of the class had to look as well, just to check to make sure there wasn't someone there.

33

By the time he was standing in line in the cafeteria, it had become obvious to Justin that most of the kids avoided him not because he was being ostracized but because they were afraid of him. He got his food and chose to sit at a table by himself, and a few minutes later Tim came and slid into a chair next to him.

Justin remembered being confused by the fact that Tim seemed almost nervous when delivering his message. But now there was nothing confusing about it. It made sense to him because Justin had discovered that his anger was like a bullet constantly looking for a target. And Tim knew that by sitting down next to Justin, he was presenting himself as a target.

"Come to steal my lunch money?" Justin asked, and there was a mocking undercurrent to his question. When Justin had still been part of the gang, he and Billy had seen the movie *The Godfather* and had decided to extract protection money from the freshman boys. They decided that every week a different member of the gang would go around and collect. It had become a great joke with them that Tim hadn't managed to get a single penny when it was his turn to collect.

Tim laughed nervously. "Gimme a break, Justin." He tried to say it lightheartedly, but it was almost an appeal.

It was an appeal that Justin could hear but knew he wouldn't respond to.

Tim continued, "Listen, I'm just here to give you a message from Billy."

"Why? He can't speak for himself?"

"He wants to talk to you, but every time he tries—"

"I'm here now, and he can say whatever the hell he wants," Justin retorted. "So where is he?"

At that moment Billy appeared at the doorway to the lunchroom.

"There he is," Justin said, half-rising from his chair.

"Wait," Tim hurried to explain, "I mean he wants to talk to you, but not now. Later. During last period, around three thirty, at the back stairwell near the gym."

As Justin watched, he saw Billy's brother, Zack, sneak up behind and try to get his brother in a headlock. Billy twisted out of it, and in retaliation gave his brother a playful shove.

The sight of that made Justin feel . . . he didn't even know what. Empty. Desolate. Wild.

"If he wants to talk to me, he can talk to me now," he said, almost breathless with anger. He started toward Billy.

"Justin, no . . ." Tim reached out and grabbed his arm, but Justin's look when he turned around made Tim drop his hand as if he had touched a live burner on a stove.

"I think you'd better stay out of it," Justin said.

Then he turned his attention back to Billy, who was still roughhousing with his brother. They were both laughing. They didn't notice Justin approaching—until he stopped a few feet away and spoke.

"Hey, asshole."

Billy looked up. When he saw who it was, he let go of his brother and stepped forward, putting himself between Justin and Zack.

"You wanted to talk to me?" Justin demanded.

"Yeah, but *later*," Billy said.

"If you have something to say to me, you can say it now."

Justin could hear his voice getting louder. Kids at the tables nearby turned to see what was happening, and Billy's gang, most of whom had been seated at a table a little ways away, headed over toward them.

But it was Zack who stepped between them.

"Let it go, Justin," Zack said, and there was the tone of command in his voice.

At least Zack wasn't scared of him, Justin thought, with the most unexpected feeling of gratitude.

It might have ended there, but Billy ruined it. He quickly pulled his brother back. "You stay out of this, Zack," he said urgently, as if Zack were in some sort of imminent danger.

That's when Ricky grabbed a bottle of ketchup off the table and darted forward, squirting it on Justin's shirt. "Murderer," he said in a mock-hysterical voice. "Look, he's got blood all over him. He's a psycho murderer."

Justin looked down at himself, and the sight of the splattered ketchup brought back that other image. He remembered what it had been like to be covered in a fine mist of his brother's blood. At that moment in the cafeteria, covered in ketchup, Justin thought he experienced something of what a murderer might feel.

Billy stepped up, obviously intending to try to keep Justin from tearing Ricky apart. But at that point, in Justin's rage-filled world, Billy was just as good a target as Ricky. Better even. The rage was like a fire that burned his brain clean of thought, and he lashed out viciously. Billy caught him in a clinch, and they crashed to the floor together.

The very intensity of Justin's response ignited some sort of primal instinct in the boys who crowded around them. There was a shrill, almost frenzied pitch to their yelling. Justin could hear the noise, and he gave in to the blissful release of striking out. Even when Billy fell on top of him, Justin continued pummeling Billy in the body. He did nothing to protect himself, so when Billy let go and started hitting back, the blows landed on Justin's face. The first split his lip. The second connected with his jaw, and his head snapped back, cracking sharply against the concrete floor. He didn't exactly black out. Rather, everything went white. It was as if the fluorescent lighting suddenly took on the brightness of a nova.

34

Justin blinked—and found himself sitting outside the principal's office. The blinding intensity of the pain dulled suddenly to a throbbing ache that pounded through his head. He looked up and saw that Mr. Franks was opening the door to his office. The principal half-turned and laid his hand on Billy's shoulder. "You're doing just fine," he said.

Billy glanced over at Justin. "Thanks, Mr. Franks," he said, obviously uncomfortable. "Can I go?"

"Yes, you can go now, Billy."

Billy fled.

Then the principal turned to Justin, and his face creased into a frown. He opened the door a little wider and said, "Justin," and it was both a command and a reprimand.

Justin got up and followed the principal into the office. He sat in the chair that Billy had occupied a few moments before, sliding down so he was slouched as low as he could manage—as if by this method he could somehow disappear under the principal's radar.

There was a long, heavy silence.

Finally the principal spoke. "So, here we are again," he said, stating the obvious.

Justin always marveled at how good adults were at being able to speak without actually saying anything.

Mr. Franks went on, in a kinder tone. "Look, is there anything you want to say to me before we get into this?"

Justin didn't even look up, much less respond—not because he was angry, but really because he had no idea what to say. How would he start? How could he explain what he didn't understand himself?

The principal waited a moment, then sighed.

"Justin, we can't have this kind of thing, you know. You can't attack other students. That's just not acceptable."

"But he came after me," Justin protested. It was exactly what he'd said the other times, but this was the first time that, as he said it, he knew it wasn't true. Billy had been the one to grab him, but only to keep him from going after Ricky. So Justin didn't feel the same swell of bitterness and injustice when Mr. Franks shook his head and said, "There comes a time when you have to take responsibility for your actions. I want you to promise me you're going to leave Billy alone."

"You want me to leave him alone, huh?" Justin repeated.

"Will you?"

Justin opened his mouth to say he would, but instead he found himself saying sarcastically, "I guess he'd better stay out of my way."

That's when Mr. Franks started to lose his temper. His lips thinned as he said, "I've tried to make allowances for your situation, but there comes a point when allowances turn into excuses."

Justin gritted his teeth to keep from yelling back at him—to keep from asking him, at what point did you get over your brother getting his brains blown out so they splattered all over you?

Right after the accident Justin had become obsessed with war films: *Platoon*, *Apocalypse Now*, and *The Thin Red Line*. His parents were disturbed by this and tried to stop him. They didn't understand. How could they? It hadn't happened to them. When he watched the movies, he felt like those guys would understand how he felt. They'd had their best friends blown to pieces in front of them. At fifteen he had had an experience that most people never have in a lifetime. And the principal was sitting there telling him that at a certain point you had to get over it. Somehow Mr. Franks had decided that a year was supposed to be enough time. Justin didn't know if a lifetime would be enough.

The principal must have realized his mistake. Maybe he read

Justin's face, maybe he just realized how what he said had actually sounded, because his next words were milder.

"You know what I don't understand? You and Billy used to be friends."

"Things change," Justin said.

"I hope things will change for you, too. They have to change. It can't go on this way. I sympathize, but I can't have you doing this kind of thing repeatedly in this school. Either you shape up or you're out. Do you understand?"

"I don't believe this," Justin said bitterly. "This is so unfair."

"Life's not fair," Mr. Franks said, but gently. "We all want to help you, Justin."

"What do you want to help me with?"

"We want to help you move past this," Mr. Franks said.

Finally Justin allowed himself to say what he was really feeling. "Move past this?" he practically spat. "How the hell am I supposed to move past it? It happened. It's not about to go away."

"It happened a year ago," the principal pointed out.

"Yeah. To the day."

Mr. Franks looked up sharply.

"It was a year ago today?"

Justin shrugged.

"I didn't realize it was a year ago today," the principal said. "Is there a memorial service?"

"Yeah. My parents are having something."

"I didn't hear . . ."

"They didn't want to make a big deal of it," Justin said. Thank god, he thought. He remembered the actual memorial as if it had happened yesterday. It was like a circus. Hundreds of people had come. Everyone from Mark's class. His teachers. Most of Justin's class and his teachers. It was like a nightmare. He'd felt everyone sneaking glances at him, trying to see how he'd hold up. He knew they were wondering how he could look so calm. He didn't tell anyone that he felt frozen. Numb. He felt like he could have put his hand in a fire and he wouldn't have felt a thing. Not even a trace of heat.

"I'm sorry. I didn't know," Mr. Franks said again.

"Yeah. Can I go now?"

Mr. Franks said, almost humbly, "If that's what you want."

Justin got up to go. He had just reached for the handle of the door when Mr. Franks spoke again. "I'm sorry if I was hard on you."

Somehow that was just too much. Justin couldn't take the sympathy. It seemed to release the huge ocean of emotion that he was barely managing to keep contained.

He turned back and gave the principal the finger.

Then he pulled open the door . . . and stepped straight into the prop room behind the auditorium. It felt as if everything were unraveling—and being knit together at the same time. The day was accelerating now. He was hurtling toward the end at terrifying speed.

The door swung closed behind him, and he turned to face the room filled with junk from a hundred different high school plays. He rounded a clothes rack packed tightly with old, molding costumes. There were seventeenth-century doublets and hose shoved up against flapper dresses and zoot suits.

Once he squeezed by the clothes rack, he immediately caught sight of Megan. She was perched on the arm of an old sofa—just sitting there, head bent, her hair half-falling around her face. Justin stood there quietly for a moment, watching her.

She must have sensed something, because at that moment she looked up. When she saw him, she stood abruptly, then didn't seem to know what to do with herself.

"Hey," she said awkwardly.

He could feel almost tender toward her when she wasn't looking at him, but the second she looked at him, he felt incredibly self-conscious under her gaze.

"Hey," he said, but in a clipped, cold tone.

She looked down again, and bit her lip. But she valiantly tried again. "Thanks for coming to meet me."

"Yeah." He hesitated. "So what do you want?"

His words were rude, but he somehow managed to say them in a milder tone.

She looked pathetically grateful for that little consideration.

"I . . . well . . . I mean, I remembered that today . . . that today . . ." She faltered and trailed off, looking down at her feet again.

She looked so sad. And upset. And pretty at the same time. Without even thinking, Justin took two steps forward and kissed her. And it made him think of the time when he thought kissing could make up for everything that could possibly go wrong. He wanted that to be true again. He tried to make it true by kissing her harder, by holding her tighter, but Megan finally struggled and pushed him away.

She tried to make a joke out of it, saying, "So you missed me too?"

"Sure," he said, trying to pull her back to him.

But she fended him off with her words. "'Cause you were really awful to me. Don't you want to say you're sorry?"

Justin drew back. "You want *me* to say I'm sorry?"

"Yeah. I didn't do anything. *You're* the one who changed. You didn't even bother to break up with me. You just stopped speaking to me. Do you know how hard that was?"

"How hard that was?" he repeated, not quite believing what he was hearing.

"I know I can't compare it to what you went through—"

"You're damn right you can't," he said.

"—but I think you should know you're not the only one with feelings. You weren't the only one who got hurt. I got hurt too."

"You didn't get hurt," he retorted. "You didn't lose a brother."

"No. But I lost you," she pointed out.

He opened his mouth to reply, but he didn't know what to say to that.

"I just want it to be like it was," she pleaded.

It seemed like everyone wanted him to suddenly revert back to normal. First the principal, now Megan.

"Just like it was," he repeated, his lip curling.

"With us, I mean."

"Okay, Megan. You want it to be just like it was," he said nastily. He grabbed her by the arms and pulled her toward him.

"Let go of me, Justin."

"You said you wanted it to be just like it was," he insisted.

"Ow. Justin, you're hurting me. Let go."

As he let go, he gave a little shove, but it was harder than he meant it to be. She lost her balance and tripped and fell. The couch was right behind her, and she landed on that instead of on the floor, but she was still shaken—and angry.

"Asshole," she spat.

He turned his back on her.

"You piece of shit. You friggin' loser," she yelled after him as he walked away.

She was still yelling as he opened the door and stepped through . . .

35

. . . into the boy's bathroom.

He was still breathing heavily as he crossed to the sinks and turned on the faucet. He splashed some water on his face and patted it dry with his T-shirt. Then he leaned over and rested his forehead against the edge of the sink, trying to fight off the sudden pressure in the back of his throat.

He jerked upright when he felt the hand on his shoulder. Spinning around, he saw it was only Daniel.

"You okay?" Daniel asked.

"What's it to you?" Justin snapped. He turned back to the sink, and busied himself washing his hands, but Daniel didn't take the hint and leave. Instead he waited a moment, then spoke again.

"Do you have history with Ms. Hines?"

"Yeah," Justin said without turning around.

"Did you do the paper?"

Justin looked over his shoulder at this. "What paper?"

Daniel gave a little laugh. "Guess not," he said.

Justin couldn't help smiling a little at that.

Then there was a moment when Justin and Daniel simply stood there. Something had shifted, just a little bit.

"What do you want?" Justin asked gruffly, but not unkindly.

"I wanted to say thanks for this morning."

"Forget about it," Justin said.

But Daniel wasn't about to let it go. He went on, "Billy and those guys are so lame. I know you used to hang with them, but"— and here he grinned to show he was half-joking—"I don't believe in holding people responsible for past mistakes."

Justin eyed him, not sure how to respond to this teasing, confident version of Daniel.

"Oh yeah?" Justin managed.

Daniel was suddenly serious. "Yeah. It's a waste of time. And you never know how much of that you're gonna have, right? Time, I mean. Everyone thinks they're gonna die in their bed when they're eighty. But you know different. You know that it can happen just like that." He snapped his fingers. "Bam. Game over."

Daniel was speaking Justin's own thoughts out loud. Justin ducked his head to try to cover the fact that the choking feeling was in the back of his throat again, along with a pressure behind his eyes. He tried to pass it off by saying sarcastically, "That is so deep."

But Daniel ignored the sarcasm and said sincerely, "I can't even imagine what you've been through. I tried to think what that would be like. To see your brother die right in front of you . . ."

What with the day . . . and what had happened . . . Justin folded into a crouch against the wall, dropping his face into his arms to hide the fact that the pressure behind his eyes had become too much.

Justin sensed rather than saw Daniel squat down next to him.

"Hey," Daniel said softly. "I think it's amazing that you're even still walking around. I think they'd have to lock me away."

This made Justin cry harder. Here was someone who didn't expect him to be back to normal, someone who understood that sometimes it got worse before it got better, someone who made him feel like it was okay to be a complete mess.

Daniel seemed to read Justin's mind with his next words. "And you know what else? I think everyone is scared shitless of you, and I don't just mean the fact that you might kick their ass. They're walking around in their little bubbles, and they don't want to think. You remind them that bad shit can happen. You remind them that sometimes it's not gonna be okay. That nothing's gonna be okay."

It was such a relief to hear the truth. Finally. Everyone else with their optimistic reassurances, their bullshit condolences, their "I know how you must feel," and their "time heals all wounds," they

119

made him feel like he was going crazy. Because it didn't fit with what he felt on the inside: that nothing was going to be the same. Ever. He couldn't go back to the safe little version of the world he'd lived in before. He buried his head deeper in his arms, and his shoulders shook.

Daniel gingerly reached out and put his arm around him.

Justin hadn't been able to cry like that since his brother's death. He'd been too numb. He'd been too angry. But now he discovered what was underneath.

Daniel sat there quietly, patiently waiting. When Justin finally raised his head, Daniel impulsively extended a hand and touched Justin's cheek. He gently wiped away the tears.

Justin didn't move.

Then Daniel leaned in, as if he were going to give Justin a kiss on the cheek. But then, on impulse, he touched Justin's lips with his own.

Justin sat absolutely still for a moment, feeling the incredible softness of Daniel's lips. They were softer even than Megan's. And Daniel smelled different. Megan was cigarettes and mints. Daniel smelled like shampoo.

Then, suddenly, Justin snapped out of his trance and jerked back. He gave Daniel a wild-eyed look.

"Sorry," Daniel said. "I didn't mean—"

But Justin didn't give him a chance to say what he didn't mean. Instead he grabbed Daniel by the shirt. His other hand was already curled into a fist, and he smashed it into Daniel's face once.

Twice.

A third time.

Daniel's nose was bleeding, his lip was swollen, there was blood all over his face, and now he was the one crying.

Justin paused, panting. "Come on," he spat, shaking Daniel by the shirt. "Fight back, you faggot."

But Daniel just sat there, sobbing. He didn't even try to pull himself away.

Justin let go, and Daniel fell back against the floor and curled into a ball as if to protect himself.

Justin stood up.

"Come on. Fight me," he demanded, aiming a kick at Daniel's back.

But Daniel just curled tighter.

"You fucking faggot," Justin repeated, making as if to kick him again.

Then Justin caught sight of one of his hands. Daniel's blood was smeared on the knuckles.

Justin turned and ran, slamming out of the bathroom and into the hall. And he would have kept on running—except that he caught sight of a clock on the wall.

He stopped abruptly.

The clock said it was three thirty.

With sudden determination Justin changed directions and headed the other way down the hall—toward the back staircase.

"It's time, isn't it?" the voice asked.

Justin just increased his pace.

"Justin?"

Yes, it's time, Justin said. *I'm going to meet him.* There was a pause, then he said grimly, *I hate his fucking guts.*

Justin rounded the corner, and sure enough, Billy was there. Waiting.

Billy barely had time to turn and face Justin before Justin grabbed him by the shirt and slammed him back against the wall.

"I'm here," Justin snarled. "So what the fuck do you want?"

Billy was momentarily speechless with surprise. Then he said, "I wanted to ask you . . ."

"What?" Justin demanded impatiently, shaking him.

"I wanted to ask if I could go with you," Billy said.

Justin loosened his hold. "What the fuck are you talking about? Go with me where?"

Billy looked straight at him. "To the memorial."

Justin let go at that point and stepped back. "How do you know about that?" he demanded.

Billy shrugged.

"I'm not going," Justin said.

"What do you mean?"

"Don't be so fucking stupid. What do you think the words 'I'm not going' mean?"

"You're not going to your own brother's memorial?" Billy was suddenly angry. "And you're calling me stupid? What the fuck is wrong with you?"

"There's nothing wrong with me," Justin said.

Billy snorted. "Yeah, you're absolutely fucking normal." He stared at Justin for a moment as if trying to decide something. Then he spoke again. "I think I know," he said.

"Know what?" Justin asked suspiciously.

"What's wrong with you—I think I know."

"You don't know shit," Justin said, but he couldn't keep the nervousness out of his voice.

Billy shook his head. "Yeah? How about this? I know you think it was your fault. You think what happened with your brother was your—"

With a cry Justin pushed Billy, and everything that Billy was saying, away with all his strength.

Billy stumbled back . . . back . . . back. He was at the top of the steps, teetering on the edge.

Once more Billy's body went sailing back into air. Once more his head struck the corner of the iron railing. Once more he landed, crashing down on the concrete steps.

Justin moved like a sleepwalker to the top of the staircase. Then he looked down.

Billy's body was crumpled awkwardly, half on the landing, half spilled over onto the next set of steps. As Justin stood there, immobile, he saw something dark start to seep from underneath Billy's head. It pooled and then started to drip down onto the next step. It was a little waterfall of blood.

Justin felt the hysteria rising. And it overflowed. He started to cry, sharp, jagged, hiccupping cries.

The bell rang—a shattering, earpiercing sound that echoed inside his head. Justin turned and ran. As kids spilled out into the hallway, they turned to stare at the sight of Justin, his face contorted with tears, stumbling down the hallway. But Justin was completely unaware of the attention he was drawing. In fact, he was unaware of anything but getting *away*.

He finally reached the entrance and pushed through the front doors of the school. It was a clear sunny day outside, an Indian summer day, with a warm breeze that ruffled his hair, but he didn't notice that, either. He just headed for the bus and climbed on. He was still crying.

The bus driver said, "Hey, kid, are you okay?"

"I'm fine," Justin choked out, and quickly passed by, going to the far back of the bus and sliding into the seat. He watched through the window as first the police cars arrived, then the ambulance, all with sirens blaring just as the bus pulled out of the parking lot.

Justin was still crying when he climbed down off the bus in front of the gates of the subdivision. He was crying as he walked along the street to his house. He was crying even harder when he let himself into his house and climbed the stairs.

He walked down the hall and stopped in front of his brother's bedroom door.

It was shut. It was always shut. Justin knew that his mother often went in and sat. His father did sometimes too. Justin never went inside. And he didn't go inside now. He simply stood there. Then he touched the door lightly with his fingertips.

He said, choking on his sobs, *No more. Please.*

"It's almost over now," the voice replied soothingly.

He continued down the hall to his parents' room to get the pills. He brought them back to his room, going into the bathroom briefly to retrieve the glass and fill it with water.

He stared at himself in the shattered mirror while the water climbed the inside of the glass. As he stared at his reflection, his crying finally seemed to ease. He went from hiccupping to deep breaths, to one big sigh.

When he looked down, the glass was full and the water was spilling over on his hand and down into the sink. He turned off the faucet, took the glass, and left the bathroom. Once he was in his bedroom, he sat down on the edge of the bed and said, *It'll be over now, won't it?*

"Yes."

He carefully shook one pill out onto his palm and swallowed it. Then a second. And a third. They went down so easy that he started swallowing them by the handful, until the bottle was empty.

Suddenly he found he was crying again.

I killed them, he whispered. *I killed them both.*

"No, Justin. The only person you really tried to kill was yourself."

But Justin wasn't listening. He was so tired. Too tired to even sit up. He lay back down on the bed, but was vaguely aware of something hard and lumpy under his back. He pulled it out from under him—and discovered that it was the remote to the television. More from habit than anything else, he flicked it on. But he didn't watch. Instead, still crying, he rolled over onto his side, curling up like Daniel had on the bathroom floor.

Justin gradually stopped crying. He didn't even feel bad anymore. All he felt was a wonderful floating feeling. His bed was a raft, and it was floating. Going out with the receding tide. Taking him with it. He was already very far away when he heard the voice of his mother. She was crying and yelling and pulling at him. Trying to roll him off the raft. Then his father's deeper voice, and his father's arms, scooping him up as if he were a baby again. He couldn't hear the words, but he knew what they were saying. They were calling for him to come back. He tried to move his lips, he tried to tell them that it was too late.

He was already gone.

36

"Wake up."

No, Justin whispered.

"Wake up, Justin."

No more, he said, keeping his eyes tightly shut. *You promised.*

"I know. I did promise. It's over."

Justin didn't move.

"It's over," the voice repeated. *"You can open your eyes now."*

Justin hesitated, then cracked his eyes open just a tiny bit.

All he could see was white.

He blinked, clearing away the tears that blurred his vision, and he could see an expanse of white ceiling—but he knew immediately that it wasn't the ceiling of his bedroom. His bedroom ceiling had a road map of fine cracks; this ceiling was smooth, recently painted. And he wasn't lying in his bed. He was lying in a big leather recliner that was leaned so far back it was almost like a bed.

"I'm here," the voice said.

The voice was different too, he realized; it wasn't inside his head anymore. It was coming from somewhere over to his right. Nearby.

"Look at me," the voice said.

Justin turned his head and looked. Then he closed his eyes again.

"Justin?" Then, more gently. "Justin. Do you know where you are?"

Justin sighed and opened his eyes again and looked at the man sitting next to him: the now-familiar lined face, the short gray hair, the military straightness with which he sat in his chair. Dr. Ryden.

"Yes," Justin said. "I remember."

A moment ago he'd lain down in his bed with the bitter taste of the pills in his mouth. But the taste was gone now. It was amazing how strong the memory had been, since it had been almost a month since he'd swallowed them. It took him a moment to reorient himself, to put together the pieces in his mind. What had actually happened right afterward? The first faint memory was a sound: the wail of the ambulance, quiet as a whisper. Then the sense of an echoing place with lots of noise and a sense of urgency so strong it managed to break through his floating peace—that must have been the emergency room. But the first *real* memory he had was of waking up in a sterile hospital room with his throat burning from the stomach pump they'd administered and an IV drip taped into his arm.

He was crying when he came to, and he hadn't been able to stop—not until they'd given him a sedative. They'd kept him in the hospital for two days before he was finally released. His parents took him home, and that had been even worse than the hospital. In the hospital there had been the sedatives and the brisk efficiency of the nurses, who stayed only long enough to give him the pill or check his blood pressure. At home he had to deal with his parents. He was always aware of their anxious, hovering presence. Their worried faces. Their nervous questions: "Do you need anything?" "Are you all right?" "If you want to talk about anything . . ." His mother was constantly on the verge of tears. Justin knew it was his fault. He knew he wasn't doing well. But it felt like it was something beyond his control. And his parents certainly couldn't help him.

So they brought him to Dr. Ryden.

Justin hadn't wanted to go. He was sure a psychiatrist would be even worse than his parents, and that Dr. Ryden would turn out to be some sappy guy who would talk to him in one of those soft, terribly *understanding* voices and would ask him about how he was *feeling*.

He couldn't have been more wrong.

Justin had gone in alone for his first appointment, leaving his mother fidgeting in the waiting room. When Justin had entered, Dr. Ryden hadn't even smiled; he'd simply instructed Justin to take a seat. Then, in a business-like voice he had told Justin about his background. He said he'd been a doctor in the army, and his specialty was treating soldiers suffering from post-traumatic stress disorder. He explained that he used hypnotherapy to bring the patient back to the time of the trauma in order to reexperience the event. He said that the standard technique was called exposure therapy where the patient simply reimagined the event, but he'd had even more success using hypnosis. However, the experience was also more intense.

"You mean it really feels like you're going through it again?" Justin said.

"We call it flooding," Dr. Ryden told him. "And yes, it feels as if you are reliving it."

"Are you crazy?" Justin said. "No way. I'm not going through that again."

"It wouldn't be today," Dr. Ryden said. "There would be a number of sessions before we actually take you back."

"I don't care if it's not for ten years. I'm not doing it," Justin declared.

Dr. Ryden stared at him for a long moment. Then he said, "But aren't you reliving it every day as it is?"

At the time, Justin had wondered how Dr. Ryden knew.

Dr. Ryden went on in a calm, unemotional voice. "Ultimately, this is your decision. It's not something I can do without your full cooperation. So I want you to think about what you are going to do about this problem if you *don't* do this technique with me. You have to decide, if not this, then what? If you want me to help you, you need to follow my instructions. Decide if you are willing to do that, and then we can proceed. If so, you can call my secretary and schedule another appointment. If not, I wish you the best of luck."

Dr. Ryden stood up, signaling that the meeting was over.

"That's it?" Justin asked.

"What else would there be?" Dr. Ryden asked.

Justin had expected that Dr. Ryden would try to convince him, and then he would be able to stubbornly insist that he wasn't doing it. But Dr. Ryden obviously wasn't planning on doing that. As Justin was leaving, Dr. Ryden asked him to send his mother in.

This was where the convincing would happen, Justin thought. The doctor would enlist his mother to persuade him.

His mother's meeting seemed to last longer than his own, and when she came out, she seemed subdued. Justin expected her to start in on him as soon as they got in the car, but she didn't say a word. Finally Justin had to ask her if the doctor had told her about the procedure. She nodded. "And?" Justin asked. She simply shrugged and said, "It's your decision."

The next day Justin asked his mother to call to schedule another appointment.

Then they began the preparation. Session after session. Talking about everything in detail beforehand. Practicing the hypnosis so that Justin would be comfortable going into the deep state that Dr. Ryden said was necessary for this kind of work.

After all the work, Justin thought he'd known exactly what to expect. But he hadn't expected this. Justin could feel that his cheeks were still wet from the tears. He reached up and rubbed them away.

"You did well," Dr. Ryden said.

As the doctor spoke, Justin could remember what it felt like to hear that merciless voice in his head—pulling out his memories, holding them up to the harsh light of truth.

"I didn't do anything. You did it," Justin responded.

"That's not true," Dr. Ryden said. "This work is easier when exploring an event years in the past, but with something as recent and as painful as this . . . often the mind simply can't handle it. You have to be very strong and very determined to get past the initial memories."

Justin thought he might even have heard a hint of emotion in the doctor's voice—something like admiration.

"Initial memories . . . ," Justin repeated. "You mean the lies?"

"No, I mean the initial memories," Dr. Ryden corrected. "They weren't lies. You see, memory is what we forget with . . . when we need to forget."

"I wanted to forget everything," Justin said quietly. "I wanted to forget I even existed."

"And you very nearly succeeded. The intern who treated you in the emergency room said it was a close thing. Very close."

They were silent for a moment.

Then Dr. Ryden asked, "And now? Do you still wish you had succeeded?"

It was a question that Dr. Ryden had asked several times over the last month. Justin's answer had always been the same: an unhesitating "yes."

He opened his mouth to respond—with the same answer, of course. But then, for some reason, he paused.

"What is it?" Dr. Ryden asked.

It was the same question Justin was asking himself. What was it? What was keeping him from answering? Then he realized.

It was because the old answer wasn't true anymore.

But even as he realized that the old answer wasn't true, Justin also knew that it didn't make any sense. But somehow, something had changed.

Justin looked up. "No," he said. "I don't."

Justin expected some sort of reaction—surprise, pleasure, satisfaction—but Dr. Ryden simply nodded.

"So," Justin asked after a moment. "What now?"

"I think you might be ready," Dr. Ryden said.

Justin felt a sudden tightening in his chest. "Ready for what?"

"Ready to go back."

Justin knew immediately what Dr. Ryden meant, but he said, "Back?"

Dr. Ryden nodded.

"When?"

Justin should have known what the answer was going to be.

Dr. Ryden looked at him and smiled a little.

"No time like the present."

37

Justin's mother pulled into the parking lot near the hill leading up to the school—exactly where the bus always stopped in the morning.

"Are you sure this is a good idea?" she asked nervously.

"It wasn't *my* idea," Justin said.

"Maybe you should wait, then."

A part of him wanted desperately to say, "Yes, maybe I should wait." But instead he shrugged and asked, "Wait for what?"

"It's the middle of the week . . . the middle of the day even," his mother said. "Maybe you want to wait till you can start fresh on a Monday morning."

"*That* doesn't make a difference," he snorted.

"Then . . . maybe you want to wait until you're a little . . . well . . . stronger."

He knew the reason she said it. He knew that she wanted to protect him, but he also knew that didn't work. Avoiding things, running away—that was what really broke you down in the end.

"It'll be okay," he said.

"If you're sure . . . ," she said, but he could hear the doubt in her voice. "Anyway, I'll be here. Whenever you're ready. I took the whole day off."

"The whole day?" he repeated sarcastically, and immediately regretted it. Justin had promised himself he'd be nicer to his mother, but he was discovering that even though life could change in a split second, changing yourself took a bit longer. The problem was, he was so used to trying to hurt her, and he knew just how to do it.

"I'm thinking of quitting," his mother said, her voice thick. "I've been thinking of it for a while."

"No," he told her. "I don't want you to quit."

"But then I could be there for you."

"I'm okay. Really."

"I should have been there for you," she insisted.

He shook his head. "It's okay."

"No, it's not okay," she said fiercely. "I should have *been* there."

And Justin knew she wasn't talking about being there for him. She was talking about before. She was talking about Mark. He also knew well what she was thinking: If only she'd been home. If only she had been there and had let Mark watch his show. Or even if she hadn't let him watch his show, if she'd been at home, he wouldn't have been able to go into the bedroom—and then he wouldn't have been near the gun. And then it couldn't have happened.

Probably on another day it would be another avenue of regret—like if only they hadn't bought the gun. If only they hadn't kept it loaded. If only they hadn't kept it right there next to the bed. As parents they should have known better than to keep a loaded gun in the house with two boys. But Justin remembered, even if his mother didn't, that she'd bought the gun after the news story about the girl who had been kidnapped from her bedroom in the middle of the night. His mother had bought the gun, and undoubtedly had decided to keep it loaded and close at hand, in an effort to try to prevent a different threat. The problem was, there was simply no way to foresee and prevent everything.

Justin knew what his mother was doing—because he'd done it to himself. What if . . . ? What if . . . ? What if . . . ? He'd imagined a dozen different scenarios, but he'd been aware they were all fantasy. He'd always known exactly what had happened. *That* event, at least, he recalled clearly. In fact, he remembered it as if it had been branded into his brain. He had been lying there on the bed when Mark pulled out the gun . . . and he hadn't done a thing. He hadn't even tried to get the gun away from Mark. In fact, he hadn't moved except to reach for another handful of potato chips—his mouth had been full when he'd replied to Mark's threat to "kill the kid" by saying, "Be my guest."

133

Afterward he, too, had gone through the "what-ifs." What if he had done something else? What if he had at least tried to get the gun away from Mark? What if he had managed it? But whatever scenario he came up with during the daytime to change the course of events, that night he would dream it, but in the dream the ending was always the same. Mark always died. It was Justin's brain telling him that no matter how many different ways you imagined it, you couldn't change it. All you could manage to do was torture yourself.

Like his mother was doing now.

"It wasn't your fault," Justin told her, even though he knew it wouldn't do any good. He knew the door of that particular prison could only be opened from the inside. He could see the futility of his words in the sad smile she gave him.

He sighed. "Well, I guess I'd better go."

"I'll be here," she said.

38

Justin climbed the hill slowly and pushed open the swinging door at the entrance to the school.

It had been only a month, but in some ways it felt as if he had been gone for years and was now returning to a place that seemed more part of his dreams than part of reality. The long corridor stretched out before him, and it wasn't packed but kids were milling around, digging books out of their lockers or standing in little clusters. It must be the end of lunch, he realized.

He stood a moment, taking it all in. He had never been so aware of the smell before—a mix of wax and musty old books and fried food. There was also the strange quality of the sound in the hallway; the ring of voices sounded almost hollow. As he listened, he realized that the metal from the lockers sent the sound bouncing around, and there was actually a slight echo. You only heard it if you listened really closely. But it was there.

As he started down the hall, he knew that some kids were looking at him and whispering. But now he could see that there were a lot who didn't even notice him.

Then he saw a familiar figure. Or he thought it was familiar. He could only see the person's back.

He approached, but he felt disconnected from his legs and feet—as if they were moving, taking him closer, against his will.

Then the familiar figure turned around.

It was Billy.

Justin saw with horror that there was a line of blood dripping down his forehead from underneath his hair.

"Dr. Ryden?" he whispered, half-expecting the doctor's voice to answer him in his head.

But the voice, when it came, rang out from behind him.

"Look who's here," Ricky called out. "Psycho killer is back." Then Ricky started singing the old eighties tune, "Psycho killer. Fa fa fa fa fa fa—" But Ricky didn't get to finish.

Without even thinking—at the sight of that trail of blood, his brain had frozen—Justin whipped around. Ricky had come up right behind him, so close that Justin couldn't even get in a full swing. That was the only reason Justin didn't break Ricky's nose, but even so, when Justin's fist connected, Ricky let out a shriek that sounded more like the squeal of a pig than a noise that came from a person.

"You hit me," he wailed. "You hit me."

"Get out of my face or I'll hit you again," Justin said, feeling a strange sense of calm.

"You're going to be in *big* trouble," Ricky said.

Justin made as if to raise his fist, and Ricky turned and fled down the hall.

"I can't believe I did that," Justin muttered under his breath.

"Why not? It's not like beating up on people is something new for you."

Justin turned.

Billy was standing behind him, scowling. Now that he was closer, Justin could see that what he had thought was a trail of blood was actually the bright red line of a scar, snaking down Billy's forehead.

Dr. Ryden was the one who had told him about Billy. No one else had thought to mention to Justin that Billy was alive. In fact, when Justin had lain there in the hospital that first night thinking he'd killed his best friend, Billy had been only one floor above him. Apparently they'd stitched up his head, taped some broken ribs, and set his arm, then kept him overnight to see that the concussion didn't develop into anything else. They'd let him go the next morning, and by the time Justin was released into Dr. Ryden's care, Billy was already back in school.

Justin took a deep breath. "You look good," he said.

"You think so? This is good?"

Justin didn't know what to say. The truthful answer was yes, Billy alive and walking around—that looked good to him. Even with a scar and a cast.

"Did you come back 'cause you wanted to break my nose, too, but you just hit Ricky by mistake?"

"No, I didn't hit Ricky by mistake," Justin said. "I hit him on purpose. But I shouldn't have done it."

"The hell you shouldn't. For the last month he's been calling me Frankenstein," Billy said, gesturing at his scar.

Justin couldn't help it. He let out a snort of laughter.

"Oh, fuck you," Billy said, but Justin thought he might have detected the slightest tug at the corner of Billy's mouth.

"Sorry."

"You should be," Billy retorted.

"I am. And not just about . . . I mean . . . I wanted to—"

Billy cut him off. "I don't want to hear any bullshit apologies, okay? All I want is for you to stay away from me."

Justin nodded. "Okay. If that's what you want."

"It is," Billy assured him. Then they stood there for a moment in silence—but Billy didn't make any move to leave.

And suddenly Justin felt better than he had for a long time.

"I don't know what you're smiling at," Billy said. He tried to scowl, but he couldn't quite manage it; this time Justin definitely saw his mouth twitch.

ML   S/0